ORPHANS

ORPHANS

BEN TANZER

SWITCHGRASS BOOKS   NORTHERN ILLINOIS UNIVERSITY PRESS   DeKalb

© 2013 by Switchgrass Books, an imprint of Northern
Illinois University Press
Published by the Northern Illinois University Press,
DeKalb, Illinois   60115
Manufactured in the United States using acid-free paper.
All Rights Reserved
Design by Shaun Allshouse

Library of Congress Cataloging-in-Publication Data
Tanzer, Ben.
Orphans / Ben Tanzer.
pages cm
ISBN 978-0-87580-695-2 (pbk.) —
ISBN 978-1-60909-099-9 (e book)
1. Orphans—Fiction. 2. Fantasy fiction. I. Title.
PS3620.A725O77 2013
813'.6—dc23
2013020897

For Mark Brand,
Adam Lawrence, and
Joseph Peterson.

1

I am staring into the bathroom mirror and I am steadying myself. The fluorescent lights strung overhead are glaring and eerie: exposing every pit mark, chicken pox scar and bump on my cheeks, forehead and neck. Random cobwebs blow to and fro on the ceiling above, dancing on an unidentified breeze. I start to gear up, now bouncing on the balls of my feet, now throwing punches, now repeating my new mantra.

"Always be closing."

I watch the words form on my lips. Spittle flies. My face contorts. I can say it louder than that. It doesn't matter if I'm only saying it in my own head. I can be more amped. I can be more impassioned. I can be more convincing. It is my mantra and I need to sell it.

"Always be closing!"

Getting there, almost, but still, I can be more intense, more stoked, and I can hit it, harder, bigger. I can be a hurricane, a tsunami, an earthquake. And I can believe it, all of it. I can also believe in myself.

"ALWAYS BE CLOSING!"

I can do this. I can do this. I can do this. And I will do this. I have to do this. It's not like this is my only shot, but there are bills to pay, things that have to be taken care of, basic things—school bills, the mortgage, credit cards, groceries, haircuts, and on and on. It's about basics, survival stuff.

And the debt, the debt must be paid.

It's also about being a man, a man who takes care of his family. A man who told his wife that he could be a provider and that they should keep their baby, even if they can only have one. I want, no, need to prove to her, to society, to myself, that I am that man. That even in a world where work is so sparse, where money is limited and the Corporation rules and where my son now studies Mandarin in school, a man can still do what men do, and this man is going to do it. I am tired of sitting down at the kitchen table every night and talking about which bill should be paid this week, and how that will be possible when there is no money.

I will not be a bum. This is my shot. I look in the mirror one more time at my newly coiffed hair, my clean shave and my eyes—my almost, but not quite sunken eyes that want to recede somewhere deep into my skull and hide from all they do not want to see.

"Always be closing!" I shout again, listening as the words bounce around my worried brain like a pinball. And then I walk out into the conference room to meet my client, her long shapely legs poking out from the table, her skin as blue as Neptune, though I hope not nearly as cold to the touch.

2

As the sun slowly comes up over Kanas Lake, orange and runny, like a cosmic egg yolk spreading across the sky, I arrive back home. The automated 24-hour doorman meets me as I walk into my building. We live in a high-rise in what used to be known as the Gold Coast neighborhood in what used to be known as the city of Chicago. It was known as the second city then, but things change, and with loans past due and naming rights one of the few options left, the neighborhood is now known as Sector Six, or Lee-Oh, in all legally binding documents, and Happiness in the real estate ads. The city itself is now known as Baidu, though people still meet at Jiaboa Plaza on the first Thursday of each month to protest the name change.

"What up, E.C.," I say to the doorman—"E.C." being short for "electronic concierge," so lifelike and yet not: too perfect, too polite, always happy and, even with advances, ultimately robotic in manner.

E.C. is parked behind a stainless steel desk, which sits on a stainless steel floor and is surrounded by stainless steel walls. It was all once slick and modern, but now it's dull with no hope of being anything but that.

"Hello Mr. Radd, how are you sir?" E.C. asks.

"Please don't call me sir," I say, "Norrin is fine."

"Yes sir," E.C. responds.

"What do I need to know?" I ask.

"Well sir," E.C. says looking down at the console on the front desk, "Joey is awake and watching television in the living room and Shalla is still asleep."

"Yeah, how does she look?" I ask, thinking about how stunning Shalla is to watch as she sleeps, her cocoa hued skin nearly glowing and her long, dirty-blonde hair flowing across the pillows like a vision from another world.

"Pardon sir?" E.C. asks.

"Never mind, I'm going to run upstairs now."

"Excellent sir," E.C. says, "and would you like me to start your coffee?"

"Please, it's been a long night."

As I ride up on the elevator the Xinhua News Agency news splashes across the back of the door. Not that I pay attention. Work, family, debt, work, family, it's all I care about now.

I walk down the hall to the apartment and quietly open the door so as not to startle Joey. I walk into the living room and watch him as he watches television, seeing a small grin creeping across his beautiful still waking-up face, his caramel skin soft and flawless, his honey-colored hair sticking-up in a dozen directions, his little arms and legs splayed across the couch and poking out from his almost too small Sanmao pajamas. Joey yawns and as he stretches his arms he notices that I am watching him.

"Daaaaaaaaaaady!" he screams, throwing his arms in front of him gesturing for a hug.

I bury my face in his awesome five-year-old neck and nuzzle him there until he pushes me away. I quickly wipe away the tears that have appeared with such a sudden ferocity and take a long look at him. The idea that Shalla and I could have created something as perfect as this child nearly breaks my heart. It's at these moments that I remember why I am doing the things I do, so that he can have a different, better life than I have had and will have.

I am also reminded though that it is moments like this

that make parenting possible, that while parenting can feel like a trap and is so often fraught with anger, pain and frustration there are moments like this—sporadic bursts of joy and peace and love—that cancel out all of the other stuff.

"What did you get me?" Joeys asks shaking me free from my embarrassing reverie.

"What did I get you—what makes you think I got you something?" I say smiling.

"You have to," he says.

"I do, why?" I ask.

"Because you're the dad, and dads get things, it's your job, duh," he responds.

"Oh, I thought my job was protecting you from monsters, but okay, how does some astronaut ice cream sound," I say reaching into my pocket for the package of freeze-dried ice cream I got him.

"Cool, can I eat some now, please," Joey says.

"Sweetie," I say, knowing what a mistake I've made even showing it to him, "it's so early, you can't eat ice cream in the morning."

"Pleeeeeeeeeeeeeeeeeeease?" he shrills like a wounded bird.

"No," I say trying to sound firm.

"Please. Now. C'mon. When will it not be morning?" he says smiling his crooked little smile.

"No," I say again though I can feel myself wavering.

"Mommy would let me have it. This is the worst day ever. I hate you," he says.

What was that about sporadic bursts of joy?

"Pleeeeeeeeeeeeeeeeeeeeeccccccceeease!" he shrieks.

"Fine, one bite," I say, knowing I do not have the strength to take on this battle.

"No, two," he replies.

"None then," I say.

"Okay one," he says.

"Hey, let's go get some breakfast before school," I say mussing his hair.

We walk down the hall to the elevator and head down to the lobby.

"Good morning Joey," E.C. says.

"Good morning E.C., look I have astronaut ice cream," he says waving the package of freeze dried ice cream he has nearly finished.

"I know," E.C. says, "and I thought your father said only one bite?"

"Whatever E.C., see you later," Joey says running ahead of me and out of the building.

"The waves look good sir," E.C. says to me.

"Yeah, how did you know I was thinking about hitting the beach this morning?"

"I know everything sir. Your kite-board will be ready when you get back."

We leave the building and Joey and I start walking to the diner.

"So, yesterday Logan said you don't have a job," Joey says, "he said he heard his mom talking about you and mommy, but I told him that wasn't true. I told him you were an astronaut, right?"

"Sure honey, that's right," I say, "I am like an astronaut."

"Cool," he says.

Here in central Baidu it's like the Emerald City. The neighborhoods may be old and in need of refurbishment, but the streets are spotless. Pristine. And unmarked. The Corporation sees to this. Cleanliness is orderliness. This changes as you make your way out toward the lake. No one bothers to clean out there. But here, no way; dirt/disorder is not allowed, not possible.

The wind picks up and my hair starts to lift off of my neck. Joey starts to shake as the whirring of helicopter blades picks up as well, first from somewhere distant, but soon right behind us.

A homeless guy approaches. I'm surprised to see him this far from the lake.

"Anything please," the homeless guy says crossing well into my personal space, "I haven't eaten in days."

He smells so rank, I don't know how even he can bare it, and I try not to make eye contact as I hand him some change.

"That's all you have," he says, "I know you have a job, you must have a job."

He pushes even closer to me in what at first feels like a threatening manner, but he's no threat, in fact he's crying, and the guilt alone is heartbreaking.

The black helicopter swoops in directly overhead.

"Please move along sir," a voice from the helicopter squawks. "And please return to the beach now."

The homeless guy backs up and looks up toward the helicopter, one hand blocking the wind from his face. He looks like he's about to say something, but then lowers his head and walks off.

I hustle Joey into the diner and get him into a booth.

"Why are there helicopters, daddy?" Joey asks.

"We talked about this honey," I reply, "they are here to protect us and keep us safe."

"From bad guys?" he asks.

"Exactly," I say. Hoping to move on I ask him, "Now, what do you want to eat?"

"So homeless people are bad guys?" he says.

"No sweetie," I say, "they're stuck in a bad situation and they don't know how to get out of it."

"Well, Logan says…"

"Let's start by not talking to Logan anymore, okay, he's dumb," which gets a laugh, "and please let me know what you want to eat."

I look around the nearly empty diner. All the diners are hunched over their food, looking to eat and get out.

"That guy's a Terrax over there, isn't it," Joey says pointing to a guy eating at the counter.

"Don't point," I say poking him in the chest, "it's not polite."

"I'm just saying," he says. "He's not really real is he?"

I take a longer look. He's probably right. The guy's skin is too smooth and too dull, he is lifelessly alive.

Joey starts to point again and when the guy sees this, he pulls his hat down over his eyes, throws some money on the counter and quickly exits.

"I knew it," Joey says triumphantly.

"It's still not polite to point," I say.

I look out the window and a dozen people dressed head-to-toe in black suddenly and furtively gather on the sidewalk. For a moment I'm struck by how completely bizarre this is, people in groups of any kind, anywhere, for any reason, but I soon realize they are part of the new flash mob movement, gathering sporadically and unexpectedly to flout the Corporation's rules against gathering of any kind.

They are standing motionless—not moving, not breathing, like statues—and they don't move or breathe until the black helicopter returns at which point they immediately disperse in different directions.

"Let's go to school," I say to Joey.

When we get to the school I walk Joey to the door and watch as he enters his cubicle and puts on his headphones. I then watch him for a moment as he begins his lesson.

"ei, bi, xi…"

3

I walk out toward the lake, my board and kite tucked under my arm. No one comes out this way anymore. The spotless streets give way to rubble, empty buildings, dirt and decay, though let's call it what it is, neglect. No one cares about the outer rings of Baidu, not beyond ensuring stability, control and calm. Always calm.

The homeless have been banned from the central city and have taken to building an extended camp that stretches along the beach, which is where I find myself now, walking out onto the beach and toward the waves.

I dodge the occasional bonfire, generator and shopping cart, weaving between the shacks and tents covering nearly any and all open space. Here and there is movement and shadowing figures flitting about, drifting from one hovel to the next, a child or dog picking through the mounds of garbage that dot the landscape. But mostly it's quiet—the real action at night, when the people who live out here feel safe enough to come outside, search for whatever they need and interact with one another.

I work my way to the last row of shelters and knock on the door of a windowless hut—half plastic, half driftwood held together by duct tape and bungee cords.

"What? Go away. Fuck off," a voice says happily from inside.

"Hey," I say, "it's me Norrin."

The door opens and out walks Lebowski, long-haired and grizzled, drink in hand. Lebowksi, real name unknown, and unnecessary out here, is the unofficial mayor and gatekeeper for the beach. Nothing happens here, not even kite-surfing, without his permission.

"Norrin Radd, how you doing?" Lebowski says, "you haven't been around much brother."

"I'm working now," I say.

"What? How? You win the lottery?" Lebowski asks laughing.

"Sort of," I say, "I submitted an application when they said they were hiring for the real estate team. I don't know how I got picked, and I didn't ask."

"And there is no reason to ask," Lebowski replies, "you just might get an answer you don't want to hear."

I'm not sure how to respond to this, not sure if there is more to his statement. It doesn't matter how long I've known Lebowski, I still don't know anything about him. He's in charge and I come here to pay my respects, because that's how it works.

"Anyway, work is a cause for celebration, hold on a moment," Lebowski says walking back into the hut. He re-emerges with two chairs and a bag full of SynthKhat, which has all of the benefits of khat, but none of the need to actually grow it. It is all synthetic. It is all lab made. And it is beautiful.

"Nice," I say.

"Well, all sorts of things wash-up on the shore," Lebowski says, "go ahead take some."

We sit down and start chewing on the SynthKhat. At first I feel nothing, but soon enough I am twitchy and euphoric watching the helicopters swoop in and out like large black gnats as the vast expanse of grey sky endlessly spins around them.

"Hey, by the way," I say to Lebowski before I head out to the surf, "I saw one of your guys out by the diner near my place this morning."

"Yeah," Lebowski says with a slight grimace, "that's not cool, did he bother you?"

"No," I say, "it was nothing, he just wanted some money."

"And you say he was one of my guys?" Lebowski asks.

"I think so," I respond, "he looked homeless, didn't smell good, you know, the usual."

"I don't think he's one of ours yet," Lebowski says, "and I don't know how we missed him, but he should know better."

Lebowski snaps his fingers and this hulking dude with a large, furry beard, wearing a leather vest emerges from behind the hut. Lebowski whispers in his ear and he takes off with a grunt.

"Hey," I say, "you're not going to do anything to him are you? He's just desperate and hungry and maybe he really doesn't know better? Who sees this kind of shit coming, right?"

"Don't worry so much," Lebowski says smiling, "we're going to take care of him, that's what we do here."

I want to believe this. I need to, too much to think about otherwise, and too high to want to anyway.

"Alright, look bro," I say looking away and toward the water, "I'm hitting the waves before my buzz wears off, cool?"

"Of course," Lebowski says, getting up and ambling into the hut, "go forth and prosper."

And so I do.

I push out into the surf, lying on my board, one stroke after another, and head toward the horizon, always wondering what lies out there, and beyond the end of the world as I know it.

Soon I see some other surfers zipping around, looking for wind and grinning maniacally when they catch a break caused by the blades of the black helicopters swooping in like seagulls looking for food.

After I go as far as I think I should—Lebowski and the tent camp just specks along the shore—I stop and sit, staring off into the cosmos, waiting for some wind and something to happen.

Eventually some wind comes in from way out on the furthest reaches of my sight line. I hesitate to jump on it, believing something better will come, looking, waiting and looking, and then with my kite suddenly, and severely, in full bloom, I'm on my feet, twitchy and trippy, and feeling like a god.

It's true that I am not an astronaut, though at one time I thought I might be. I am not even a good husband or father, but for this moment, gliding here toward the shore, weaving this way and that, and hopping from wave to wave, I am something great, even if I have no idea exactly what that is.

4

I shake the water out of my hair as I walk back into the apartment. My hope is to catch Shalla still in bed, wrapped-up in the sheets, warm and cozy, and dreaming happy dreams about a life she wants and a world she wants to live in. One that includes me, and our love, triumphant and real, and bigger than the day-to-day concerns that dog us as we manage stress and fear, and hope for something more than what we've been handed so far.

But that's the reality and I am interested in the dream—the dream where Shalla is happy I'm home and is looking forward to wrapping her arms and melting her legs around me. Her lovely hair floating like tendrils as we make love throughout the morning with the reckless abandon we knew as a new couple—wildly in love and crazy from the excitement of the unknowns still to be explored, the past we were running from, and the moment-to-moment goodness of having someone who wants to be with you unconditionally, no strings, no agendas and no confusion.

Shalla is not in bed though. She is at the kitchen table. Drinking coffee and staring off into space, as beautiful as ever, but no craziness, not the good kind of craziness anyway, in sight.

"Hey Norrin," she says sleepily as I walk over and give her a kiss, first on the cheek, lingering for a moment in her caramel awesomeness, before moving to her lips and thinking about more, always more.

If it isn't true that every time a male kisses his lover he is wondering, hoping it will evolve into sex, it would be hard to convince me of that right now as I drift down her neck to her chest, her stomach, between her legs, before we wrestle each other to the ground—a tangle of spinning, twisting arms and legs and heat and contact.

Moments later, and too soon, always too soon, we lay there staring at the ceiling, catching our breath and waiting for someone to say something.

"Wow, miss me much?" Shalla says breathlessly, small drops of sweat on her upper lip mingling with the freckles in the space below her nose that my grandmother always claimed was where God touched us before we entered the world.

"I always miss you," I say, "any time we're apart."

"Right, look dude," Shalla says grinning, "we already had sex, well, if that's what you want to call it. No need to sweet talk me anymore. We're cool."

"I was laying the groundwork for later," I say grinning back, "plus, I do miss you when we're not together. I have abandonment issues."

"Oh, I know sweetie," she replies rolling up onto her elbow. "Your daddy left you as a boy, no wait, he was snatched, right, leaving you and your mom to your own devices before she finally offed herself and you came and found me?"

I flinch. I know she's trying to be cute here, funny, right, but is it something crueler, an intention to hurt, maybe subconscious, maybe not?

"Norrin, come on, I was just messing with you," Shalla says. "I don't know what that was, really, I'm sorry."

I should move on, the comment means nothing to me, but the feeling behind it, why so much anger?

"Snap out of it," Shalla says. "What, we can't joke around anymore? Tell me about the gig and how much you got paid."

"It was cool, and I can tell you more, but first you need to know something, they didn't pay me. They said the whole thing was a simulation, a practice run and they were just assessing my potential. If they like me there will be more training and more work, paying work, to come."

"What? They didn't tell you that before you went, did they?" Shalla says almost shouting.

"No," I say weakly, "they didn't, but I will find out more when I go in for my review."

"Fuck, Norrin, we have bills to pay, school, food, fuck," Shalla says.

"That's not fair," I say, wishing that bills were our only concern.

"No, what's not fair is that you said I should keep the baby, and I love Joey, but Jesus, there was no rush, we barely knew each other, we didn't have jobs, and you didn't care, you said it would be fine, you said you needed this. Fine, make it right, go, make it right," Shalla says gathering her robe around her neck and leaving the room.

Welcome home.

5

I roll off of the train at BeiShan, the stop once known as Belmont, where I need to make a quick detour before heading into the office. This was the block where Shalla and I first met—young punks full of rebellion and anger, fleeing a world that seemed broken and never likely to be fixed. All we wanted to do then was make music and be like the Ramones—funny and abrasive, slamming and sneering, two minutes of ferocity at a time.

If it was true that my head was in the stars much of the time then too, it was because until then I had assumed that exploring space, surfing the universe and searching for new planets and forms of life was going to save me. I was never going to space though—wrong family, wrong background, just wrong, all of it.

But music was different. No one can take music away from you: they can't control it. So we dreamed about it, and chased it, ate it, slept it and loved it more than anything, until Joey. Joey changed things, and maybe it's true that I forced it, but when the music wasn't playing and the stars seemed really far away, what else did I have?

Nothing. Shalla, maybe, but love is so ephemeral, relationships implode, and was she never even mine to begin with? It was never clear. And still isn't.

I start moving along BeiShan, the level of grime coating everything from the ground to the air itself.

"Hey, fuck head, yeah, you, douche bag, over here," someone screams from across the parking lot at the Simao donut shop where we once wiled away endless days chewing SynthKhat, talking music and begging for change.

It's Al B, an old member of the band and just who I was looking for. I take a moment to catch my breath and steel myself for the conversation.

"Look at you motherfucker," Al B says charging toward me and leaning in to give me a hug, "all spiffy and proper. Is that how they make you dress when you go to work at the Corporation? Because if it is, no thanks man, this guy will pass."

After the hug I step back and take look at Al B's grungy black shorts and thermals, the ratty hoodie and unshaven face.

Is that what I used to look like?

"What, Jesus, Norrin, how bad do I look?" Al B asks.

"It's not that," I say.

"What then?" he asks straightening up. "You look like you're seeing a ghost!"

Is that it, is that what the past is when you have no true desire to revisit it? A ghost you hope will never come around even as you go and search for it.

"I suppose," I say, "how are you doing?"

"Hustling bro," Al B replies, "selling SynthKhat, playing music, keeping my head down and trying to stay one step ahead of the helicopters."

As he says this a black helicopter swoops in overhead, and hovers for a minute as the grime and grit swirls around us.

"Please move along," the metallic voice says, "per the newly revised Baidu Police Department General Order Number 00-02-2080, there is no loitering in designated hot spots."

"I should be moving," I say, "and I need to get to the office anyway, but I did want to talk to you."

"Yeah, alright," Al B says looking up and flipping the bird to the helicopter, "what's up?"

"Loitering is defined as remaining in any one place under circumstances that would warrant a reasonable person to believe that the purpose or effect of that behavior is to enable a criminal street gang to establish control over identifiable areas, to intimidate others from entering these areas, or to conceal illegal activities," the metallic voice says as the black helicopter starts to drop closer to where Al B and I are standing.

"You know what's up," I say, "the money, it's always the money."

"For you it is," Al B says laughing, "but I guess for you it should be."

"Look, he knows I'm good for it, right?" I say. "That I'm working, that I'll get it to him?"

"Oh, he knows," Al B says laughing again.

"What does that mean?" I say grabbing Al B by the front of his hoodie.

"Nothing, relax," Al B says pulling away from me, "well, not totally nothing, you'll know soon enough."

"And you know that how?" I ask.

"Bitch, I know everything," Al B says. "You should have learned that by now."

"I don't like this hanging over my head all the time," I say.

Al B shakes his head and laughs.

"Choices, motherfucker," Al B says poking his finger at me. "You made a choice, now live with it, deal, man up, it will be fine."

"Yeah, sure it will," I start to say.

"You have 30 seconds to move along," the metallic voice says, the black helicopter now hovering low enough that I can watch Al B's hair dancing on his shoulders.

"Hey," Al B says forcing a smile, but sounding sad, "say

hello to Shalla for me, please."

"Of course bro," I say, before starting to trot away, the wind initially ruffling the back of my shirt, but then moving away as I head up the street and the black helicopter flies off in search of its next intervention.

6

I slow to a walk and as I move along BeiShan toward my office. I pause to kick a bottle and as I watch it spin, it starts moving so fast I become dizzy just staring at it and have to stop for a moment to get my bearings. I place my hands on my knees and focus on my breathing, thinking about the stars and the waves and just how long it's been since I picked up an electric guitar and played it until my fingers bled and my ears buzzed from the endless distortion.

I also think about Al B as I get moving again, about choices, choosing family, what that means in terms of what you give up and how you can ever truly compare what gets lost to doing the right thing regardless?

I am snapped out of my reverie by someone shouting at me.

"You work here man?"

I look up, realize I have reached the front door of the office, and find myself standing face to face with a guy in a tattered suit.

"I said do you work here?" the guy says again, though I now realize he's not just a guy, but one of many guys all trudging down the sidewalk and heading toward me; every one of them is dressed in what remains of their once professional suits. These are guys who used to have jobs, pride and somewhere to go before the Corporation took over, the E.C.s began to replace humans and the used Terraxes were able to provide help until no longer viable.

"I do work here," I say.

"Are they hiring," he asks, "they must need some kind of help, right?"

The guy then reaches into his breast pocket and I get ready for the inevitable gun or knife. Instead he pulls out a resume, which is folded, and creased, stiff with coffee and sweat. As he goes to unfold it, a black helicopter swoops in from above.

"We will need you to disperse please, immediately," says the voice booming from the black helicopter, now so close I can feel the heat emanating from its belly.

"Fuck you," the guy screams looking up at the helicopter that remains as impassive as ever, "fuck you."

Soon all the guys are screaming "fuck you" and jumping into the air as they futilely try to grab the helicopter and bring it down to the ground.

"You have ten seconds to disperse, nine, eight...," the voice from helicopter intones, but the workers are now enraged, a maelstrom of anger, tears and frustration.

"Fuck you, fuck you, fuck you," they start to chant.

"...five, four...," the voice continues, pointlessly.

But no one is going anywhere. The helicopter rotates so one side is now facing us. A window opens and a mechanical arm holding a gun extends outward from the window and fires. The sound is so loud it echoes across the buildings and down the street like a tidal wave.

The guys in their tattered suits are now running in every possible direction. All but one anyway, because the guy who first confronted me is now lying on his back at my feet, a thin stream of blood slowly trickling from his temple, across the sidewalk and into the street.

I take a quick look and I'm struck by how still he looks, and peaceful. I hope he's in a better place, but I don't believe it.

I turn away and walk toward the front door of the office as an E.C. walks up with a crew of Terraxes to clean the sidewalk and remove the body.

7

I walk up to the office door, nondescript and hidden in plain sight. I place my hand squarely against the scanner and feel the laser glide over and around the curlicues in my fingertips and the endlessly arching cracks and folds of my palms, matching the identifying curves to the dataset that houses the handprints and DNA of all employees of the Corporation. When the green light blinks I lean forward and allow the eye scanner to pass before and across my eyes, first right to left, followed by a puff of air, then left to right, pause, another puff of air, before the scanner's beams stop to linger, boring their way into the deep recesses of my eyes.

I stand there as motionless as possible, even as my eyes begin to dry, then ache, and even as I want to close them, engulfing them in the darkness and moisture waiting there in. I have to keep them open though until the scanner is satisfied that I am Norrin Radd, no more, no less, linger, linger, green light, and the door snaps open.

I walk through the door and into the lobby.

As nondescript as the front door may be, the lobby is anything but, with its sleek, brushed-metal walls and floors, and flowers everywhere—splashes of red, blues and purples, bursts of color so intense that compared to the streets outside it's like an explosion.

As I approach the front desk, which is deep black and slick—a dark smile beckoning and repulsing me—a specially crafted office chick E.C. walks up, her skin as smooth as the walls behind her, her shapely ass on the verge of bursting the seams of a nearly too-short skirt.

Not human I remind myself. Not that people don't fuck E.C.s, they just have to be built for that. I switch gears, married I tell myself, happily married.

"Welcome to Joyful Future Real Estate," the E.C. says, "are you Norrin?"

"I am," I say smiling and leaning forward, "what gave me away, is it the chip they secretly implanted in my brain?"

"They said I should be on the lookout for someone so handsome it would take my breath away," the E.C. says.

"Imagine if you could actually breathe," I say.

"You'd be surprised," the E.C. says, "I can get breathing pretty hard when I set my mind to it. Let me know if you ever want to see that."

"I definitely will," I say, "just don't hold your breath, I'm married."

"So am I, to my job," the E.C. says suddenly breathing hard, so lifelike, but so wrong.

"I hope I will be too," I say backing up and trying to ignore my erection, also wrong, and definitely lifelike.

"You will," the E.C. says as a door not seemingly there moments before opens to the side of the desk, "you will."

I walk down a hall and head toward the coffee room. There is a table in the middle of the room, some counter space and a kitchenette. It is all standard, expensive-looking, but standard.

"Coffee, please, black," I say as I walk in, and an arm extends from the counter with a hot cup of coffee.

I take the coffee and turn my attention to the table.

Sitting around the table are two of my potential coworkers, Ricky and Shelley, and John, the boss.

"Look whose back," Ricky shouts clapping his hands, his perfect hair unmoving, his white teeth blinding everyone for a two-mile radius.

"How you doing kid?" Shelley asks, his old-man smell permeating the space between us.

"I guess we didn't scare you off?" Ricky says.

"Not this kid," Shelley says, "hell no, he's tough, cool as a cucumber, right kid?

"I'm just saying," Ricky says, "this kind of gig could have freaked him out."

"Sure, sure, of course," Shelley says, "but he's different, don't you think? He can close."

"Yeah, he can, right," Ricky says, "but it's more than closing."

"True," Shelley says, "you have to be able to handle those old space shuttles. When's the last time someone repaired one of those?"

"Turn of the century maybe," Ricky says.

"That's no good," Shelley says, "no good, and then there's the dreams, the memories, that's tough, the brain is always going."

"Well of course it is," Ricky says, "it's a long trip, it just doesn't feel like it when you're half-awake all the time. Or is it half-asleep?"

"I don't think it matters," Shelley says.

"It matters to me," Ricky says.

"Fine, whatever, let's say half-asleep then," Shelley says.

"Sure, okay, and yes there's the dome and all, but you still need to contend with the air there, so warm, hell on the hair and pores. And it's dusty too, very dusty," Ricky says.

"Well, yeah, sure it is, it's like a desert there," Shelly says.

"It's still undeveloped," Ricky says, "but not for long, right?"

"Right," Shelley says, "not if we have anything to do with it."

"You also have the Terraxes of course," Ricky adds. "And they're just supposed to fill in while you're gone. Take care of things, man stuff, walk the kid to school, shovel the driveway, fix the appliances, replacing and screwing in the light bulbs, whatever, they have to do it, it's their jobs, their reason for being."

"But that's all they screw," Shelley says, "just the light bulbs, and don't let anyone tell you different kid. Seriously, there are always stories, but that's all they are, stories. Don't let it mess with your head."

"So anyway," Ricky says, "you going to join the team or what?"

They've been talking so fast I've begun to sip my coffee and just shake my head in agreement with everything they say, concentrating instead on my kite-board, the wind and gliding along until there are no other people, and no other voices, just me and the horizon line.

"Settle down ladies," John snaps, because everything he says comes out like that. "How can anyone fucking think when the two of you are talking so much?"

"Sorry boss," Shelley says, "we're just excited to have Norrin here, fresh blood, new energy, and youth. It's something we can feed off of."

"Just don't get your panties into a bunch," John says, "we need to do his review first. Then we can decide who is joining the team and when."

Both Ricky and Shelley turn back to their coffee and I just stand there waiting for someone to tell me what to do.

"C'mon Norrin," John says motioning toward his office, "let's talk about your future, unless of course you prefer to hang out here with the coffee klatch?"

"No sir," I say walking into John's office.

8

John's office is also nondescript. I don't know what I expected, more computers maybe, blueprints, spacesuits and maps of the universe. But it's like any other office: a desk, a computer, a pencil holder and a little sign on the front of the desk, "The buck stops here and I'm the buck." It is incredibly neat, everything lined-up just so, nothing out of place, no spare papers or files lying around.

It fits John's personality though, aligning nicely with his hair, neat, clipped, short; shirts, crisp and pressed; shoes, buffed and shined; his slacks, the crease like a knife blade, ironed to the point of sharpness and slicing through the air with every step.

John and I went to high school together, something I think we both know, but have yet to acknowledge. He was an athlete and the son of a black ops space mercenary turned politician turned power broker. His dad was in early with the Chinese and now pulls strings behind the scenes, making deals and continuing the long-time legacy of Baidu politics. Fathers beget sons who assume their father's role only to at some point turn it over to their sons and on and on. I never really knew my father and so while it's clear to me how John is here, it is less so how I am. They say I got the position through the annual jobs lottery, but that still seems impossible.

"I know you are wondering how you got through the lottery," John says neutrally, reading minds apparently one of his many skills, "how a system designed to mask, conceal and otherwise obdurate the fact that all jobs are patronage jobs, spit out a plum job for a fatherless, powerless and otherwise completely unconnected citizen of a city run by and for the powerful, but the time to wonder about such things is past. You are here and your drifter, scuzzball friends like Al B are not. And yes I remember the two of you from high school, with your leather pants, spiky black-dyed hair and guitars, endlessly wandering the halls and high on SynthKhat. But that was another life. This is your new life, if you want it. Do you want it?"

"You're offering me a full-time position then," I say trying to tamp down my excitement and the idea that I will soon be able to prove myself to Shalla and pay off my debts which suddenly feel less daunting and bordering on the possible.

"That is correct, you will begin by receiving the agreed upon base salary and you will be paid a commission on all deals closed upon the signing of the required and legally binding real estate contracts. Do you have any questions?"

"I have a million of them, but I don't know where to start," I say.

"You'll figure it out and Ricky will be there to help. You start tomorrow. Be at Arthur Chin by noon to catch your flight. Good luck and welcome to the team," John says standing-up and leaning forward to shake hands.

"Tomorrow," I repeat shaking his hand, "wow, okay."

9

I practically dance down BeiShan to the train station, images of the E.C.'s metallic ass and John's words pinging around my brain. All that and possibility—because the world now feels full of possibility—wonder, adventure and security mashing together as I take care of unfinished business and see the stars all at once.

I am still dancing as I exit the train station at Dun Hwa and head toward Bao, the supermarket in our neighborhood, to buy steaks, beer and flowers.

Outside the store a Terrax is gathering shopping carts in the parking lot. As he finishes I see a guy in a suit walk up to the Terrax and shove him in the chest.

"You think you can just take our jobs you freak?" The guy screams, spittle flecking the Terrax's preternaturally calm face. "Just go the fuck away."

"I have nowhere to go," the Terrax says calmly.

"The fuck you don't," the guy says jumping on him and knocking him to the ground, his hands on the Terrax's throat, "you can go to hell."

I walk into the store and see a series of Terraxes lugging boxes and stocking shelves. They are overseen by a handful of the E.C.s, who both supervise their work and, as needed, maintain calm.

As I pick through the flowers, a Terrax next to me stops and put his hands on his hips, before bending over, then falling to the ground, motionless.

Somewhere overhead a speaker hiccups to life.

"Clean-up flower aisle, Terrax down. Repeat, Terrax down."

An E.C. walks over with two Terraxes dragging a bag behind them.

"Sorry for the inconvenience sir," the E.C. says.

"It's no inconvenience, circle of life, right?" I respond laughing to myself.

"Hakuna Matata," the E.C. says before turning his attention to the Terraxes as they fold the downed Terrax into the bag I now see is marked "Parts" and shuffle off.

I pay for my groceries and step into the alley behind the store, looking to buy a bag of SynthKhat from one of the neighborhood guys before going to pick up Joey at school.

As I close the deal a black helicopter comes in from somewhere above.

"Please disperse immediately…"

But I'm already gone.

10

"Daaaaaaaaady," Joey screams when he sees me by the door.

I drop my bags, scoop him up in my arms and as he melts into my chest I think, bursts of joy, bursts of joy, bursts of joy, savor it, hug it, love it, all of it.

"What did you bring me?" Joey says pulling away and pointing to the bags.

"What do you mean," I say, "like what?"

Joey crosses his arms across his chest and stamps his little foot on the ground. I try to keep a straight face.

"Nothing?" he says with a huff.

"How was school?" I say ignoring him.

"Nothing," Joey says, "you got me nothing? What about a snack, more astronaut ice cream?"

"Nothing, sorry dude, I thought you would just be happy to see me," I say.

"Mommy always brings something," Joey says uncrossing his arms and walking away.

"Yeah, well, mommy is the best," I say grabbing the bags.

No response. He knows that already.

"C'mon, how was school?" I shout as I run after him, "Give me something."

"Nooooooooooooooouoooooooooooooooooooo!" he says as we walk into the building, past F.C. and his queries about Joey's day, onto the elevator and into the apartment.

"Mommy, mommy, mommy," Joey yells as we walk into the living room, "look, daddy picked me up and he's got stuff."

"He does? What kind of stuff?" Shalla asks.

"I don't know," Joey says, "none of it's for me. Can I watch television?"

"Sure honey, twenty minutes though, that's it," Shalla says.

"Thirty?"

"Ten!"

"Twenty sounds great mommy," Joey says before plopping down on the couch.

The microphone on the ceiling lets out a slight metallic belch.

"What would you like to watch Joey?" E.C. asks.

"Hey E.C.," Joey says looking up at the microphone, "what's on Disney?"

"Would you prefer something more educational perhaps?" E.C. asks.

"No," Joey shouts, "I've already been to school today."

"Fine Joey, but only twenty minutes, you heard your mother," E.C. replies.

"I know, I know, good-bye E.C.," Joey says.

"See you at bedtime Joey," E.C. says.

I walk into the kitchen and the lights turn on. I stand over the stove.

"Steak, medium rare," I say and the stove begins to heat-up.

"Vase please," I say looking at the flowers, a flash of color arrayed against the once vibrant, now drab counter.

"Would you like the clear vase or the blue one?" E.C. asks as the microphone in the kitchen belches to life as well.

"Blue," I say, "thank you and if you wouldn't mind, I will need a skillet for these steaks and a bottle opener for the Tsingtao.

A slot over the stove opens up, a metallic arm extends out and a skillet is placed onto the stove. Another slot opens on the counter in front of me and a smaller arm extends out with a vase, places it on the counter, disappears back into the slot, and extends again with a bottle opener which I take.

I open two bottles of Tsingtao and turn around to see Shalla just inches away from wrapping her arms around my waist.

"What's going on?" she says.

"I got the gig. You are officially married to the newest member of the Joyful Future Real Estate sales team," I say.

"Wow, really," she says, "you got it, awesome. I'm so proud of you. When do you start, can we go do something first, I don't know, together, as a family?"

"No baby, sorry, tomorrow, I'm leaving tomorrow. Isn't that incredible," I say trying to sound positive and full of excitement about all that is to come, though not too excited, never too excited when it involves leaving.

"Yeah, that's awesome—tomorrow, okay," she says looking sad, and then recovering, smiling and adding, "let's celebrate."

"Sounds good," I say smirking, "Joey is still up though you know."

"True," Shalla says one hand on her curvy hip, "I was thinking maybe we could dance."

"Yeah, okay, that sounds like almost as much fun," I say.

"Dance, dance, dance," Joey says.

"Dance, dance, dance," I say jumping around.

"Dance," Shalla says grabbing Joey's hands and swinging him up in the air.

"Hey E.C.," I yell starting to bounce, "we need Blietzkrieg Bop."

There is a burp of electricity.

"Yes sir," E.C. replies, "enjoy."

Soon we are dancing across the living room, then po-going, higher and higher, smashing into one another until we all fall down into a sweaty, happy, smiling pile on the floor.

11

I'm falling through endless waves of red dust, never quite hitting the bottom of wherever it is I'm falling, and never quite finding balance… Suddenly there it is, the ground hurtling toward me at a speed that seems impossible to be real.

Thud.

I wake up, head pounding and confused, the room spinning. Where am I? In space, on the shuttle, what, and why is it so dark?

I slow my breathing and stare straight ahead, trying to stay calm, ride out my disorientation and wait until my eyes can adjust to the dark.

Uhhhh.

There is a moan next to me. Jesus did I kill someone?

Uhhhhhhhmmm.

I look over at the shape moving around under the covers and realize its Shalla and we're in our room and there is no great mystery here. There was the dancing, the steaks, the Tsingtao and the SynthKhat, lots of SynthKhat, and now here we are, hung over and strung out, having barely slept a wink.

Uhhhhh.

Shalla rolls over and her bare legs emerge from the sheets. They are the color of oozy butterscotch and slightly glowing in the still dark room.

I start to stroke her calves and then the pits behind her knees. She rolls away, but doesn't get very far. I grab her ankle and pull her toward me. I kiss her inner thigh, softly at first, but then more forcefully, working up toward her panties. She bends one leg and then the other, shifting and twisting, toward me, away from me. The sheets bunch-up around her waist as I keep driving forward, both fingers on the pantie's waistband. Pulling them now, tugging, Shalla inching away from them as they begin to slide down her legs, over her thighs, past her knees, down to her ankles and then on the floor. I ease her right leg over one of my shoulders and then her left over the other as Shalla grinds the back of her head into her pillow.

"Oh."

What was that, because it was not Shalla. I lift my head, but there are no other sounds. Did I really hear something? I start to bring my head back down when Shalla hits me in the shoulder. As I look up she points to the door where Joey is standing, silently and impassively, and not moving, nothing.

"Weird," Joey says.

"Hey, we're uh…," I say stumbling, unclear what lie will suffice in a situation like this.

But I don't have to respond, because Joey silently walks away toward the front of the apartment.

As I roll onto my back, shaking my head and trying to suppress a smile, I hear him say, "No E.C., nothing educational, I have school today."

Neither Shalla nor I say anything immediately, not sure what the right thing could possibly be.

"Well, I guess we don't have to be paranoid anymore about whether Joey might walk in on us some time," I finally say.

Shalla's look of horror melts into a smile.

"Which isn't going to help you get any," she says rolling over and curling up next to me.

"Really," I say, "because I always assumed that Joey

walking in on us while I was performing oral sex on you would be this tremendous turn-on. Please don't tell me I've been wrong this whole time?"

Shalla looks amused for a moment, but then quickly turns sad.

"So how long are you going to be gone?" Shalla asks.

"They say it's like four months in real time," I say.

"Why is it so long?" Shalla says.

"I don't know," I reply, "but think how long that would have taken me before they started using nuclear energy to power the space shuttles. It would have been like twenty-four months."

"That's very nice for you," Shalla says, "but I'm going to be living here with that clone the whole time; it's messed-up."

"You know, the public relations people say we are not allowed to refer to them as clones," I say. "They're purposely identified as Terraxes because that tests much better with the public. The research does show though, that Terraxes both reduce isolation and minimize the stress for the partner left behind. The Corporation takes that stuff really seriously."

"Wow, you sounded sort of smart there for a minute. Was that in the marketing materials they gave you?" Shalla says.

"Word for word," I respond, "but they really believe it."

"They just don't want to clean up any more dead bodies," Shalla says.

"That's not in the marketing materials," I say, "but I suppose you're right; dead spouses are bad for business. Meanwhile, you will be drawing my paycheck while I'm gone, no money worries, and you will have someone here to help out. That's not bad, right?"

"No, I guess its fine," Shalla says, "I just wish there was another way."

"Well, right now there isn't," I say climbing out of bed and getting dressed.

I watch her for a moment, struck by her vibrancy and hum, and the sense that, though hurting her may be the worst thing I can imagine, I am still drawn to doing so again and again.

"Hey," I say.

"Huh? What?" Shalla says half-awake.

"I saw Al B yesterday on the way to work," I say.

"Yeah?" Shalla says, pushing herself up on her elbows, "how's he doing?"

"Same, fine, I guess," I say, "I just thought you would want to know."

"Come here," she says opening her arms to me.

I walk over and we start to kiss. Shalla pulls on my belt as I fall on top of her. Soon we are lying there, spent and breathless.

"I have to fly baby," I say.

"Just remember something," Shalla says, "I chose you, not Al B. I'm not saying I didn't love him, but I had to make a choice, and this is the one I made. I'm happy with it, okay, you know that, right?"

"Yeah," I say, "I know and I love you, and I will see you soon. Right now though, I'm going to get Joey to school, hit the waves and then get to the airport, alright?"

"Alright babe, safe travels," Shalla says rolling away from me, a slight tear collecting in the corner of her eye.

Then again maybe there isn't, maybe it's just the light creeping in and playing tricks on me as the sun comes up.

12

I walk Joey to school. He is not speaking, and I wonder if I should say something about what he may or may not have seen when he walked in on us. He is staring straight ahead—no eye contact, no small talk. It's peaceful, pleasant, but I wouldn't be a parent if I didn't try to disrupt the sense of calm by asking him about something he can't possibly want to discuss.

"So, do you want to talk about that?" I ask.

Nothing. No reaction. He doesn't even look at me.

Do I jump in? Do I wait? Do I drop it? I fight the urge to push more, to address whatever guilt and confusion I am feeling by making him feel guilty and confused as well.

A black helicopter flies overhead, swoops in close to us and moves on. We walk another block in silence. I have to say something else. I will say something. I get distracted. A group of kids dressed in black run out into the street in front of us and pose as statues.

Flash mob.

I smile to myself and watch Joey watch them. He is oblivious to the fact that he is observing an effort at peaceful disobedience. Instead his beautiful face is just full of awe as he tries to absorb the randomness of a world he is just barely learning to navigate.

And then the black helicopter returns.

"Please disperse immediately," the robotic voice says.

The flash mobs always disperse, but for a moment it appears that they don't plan to, as if they truly are frozen in place. It's fantastic, until there is a loud pop.

One of the members grabs his shoulder and falls to the ground.

That pop is followed by another and another after that. The kids pick up their fallen member and run away in a variety of different directions. The helicopter hovers for a moment before flying after one part of the group.

We start walking again.

"Hey bud," I say, "do you want to talk about that, or about what you saw this morning?"

"Did you know that where you're going for work is known as the red planet?" Joey says.

"I do," I say.

"Did you know that iron is in abundance there?" he asks.

"No," I reply, "thank you for sharing that. And so we are not going to talk about this morning then?"

"No."

"Good enough."

When we get to school I give him a big hug, and while I intend to linger for only a moment, I find that I can't quite let go.

"Daddy enough," Joey says trying to wriggle free, "I can't breathe."

"Alright, sorry," I say, "I'm just going to miss you. That's all."

"Blah, blah, blah," Joey says smiling.

"Fine, get in there, go learn, and I will be home soon," I say.

I watch Joey as he walks into school, enters his cubicle and puts on his headphones. I then watch him for a moment as he begins his lesson.

"ei, bi, xi…"

After that I head back to our apartment building.

"Your kite-board is ready," E.C. says as I walk in.

"Thanks E.C.," I say, "and hey, you'll keep an eye on the family for me while I'm gone, right?"

"Yes sir," E.C. replies. "Be careful."

"Always," I say grabbing my board and heading out to the lake.

The skies are grey. There is almost no wind, except for when the black helicopters zoom too closely by. These are not ideal conditions, but I need to surf before I leave. Four months without chasing waves won't do.

I walk up to Lebowski's hut and knock on the door.

"What? Go away. Fuck off," a voice says happily from inside.

"Hey," I say, "it's me, Norrin."

"Hey kid," Lebowski says emerging from the hut, "one last ride before you head into the stars?"

"Yes, right, how did you know I was leaving?" I say.

"You know," Lebowski says waving his hands in the air as a black helicopter glides by, "you hear things. Is anything really secret anymore?"

"Good question," I say, "and yes I'm leaving today."

"How does it feel to be a suit?" Lebowski says dropping into one of the ratty deck chairs in front of his hut and motioning for me to do the same.

"I never thought of it that way," I say sitting down as well and reaching into the bag of SynthKhat that has suddenly materialized.

"Well, it is the Corporation, right?" Lebowski says.

"Sure," I say, "but isn't everything now?"

"If you choose to work," Lebowski says.

"I have to, I have my family to think about," I say recognizing I am responding defensively.

"Family first, for sure," Lebowski says, "it's like a deal with the devil I guess, right?"

My head is starting to buzz, my legs and arms limp. I want to believe it is the SynthKhat and not my fears about paying off debts, and what all that means in relation to leaving my family and Shalla, and Terraxes.

"Yeah, but the Corporation isn't all bad either, right?" I say trying to think of an argument to make, but not quite forming a cogent thought.

"Maybe, sure, okay, though I think they mostly just don't want us paying attention to what they're really up to," Lebowski says.

My head is really spinning now, everything is. It's all too much to think about.

"What are they up to?" I ask.

"You're part of it," he says. "You can't see that?"

I can't see anything, just the water, where I want to go, now.

"I'm confused," I say, "I don't know where you're going with this."

"Just think about this kid," he says. "Who's going to be leaving Baidu, and who is going to be staying here? How has the world always worked and how is it always going to work?"

"Uh, okay," I say, not quite getting it, "I think I need to go now."

"Of course, go," Lebowski says, "be good, be safe and come see me when you're back home, okay?"

"Sure," I say and as I stand up, Lebowski stands up as well and hugs me, lingering for a moment just as I did with Joey.

13

The trip out to Arthur Chin is uneventful. Bullet trains continuously run express between the airport and individual stops in the city. You step into a pod and wait for the train to approach. The train unlatches its pod filled with riders looking to exit, even as it latches onto your waiting pod, which is lowered onto the train as it reverses direction and leaves the station. Boarding is smooth, lightning fast, and in just minutes you are at the airport—no wait, no fuss.

The main entrance to the terminal is sparse, clean and well lit. There is no room for shadows, no room for error or quick moves—nothing clandestine can happen here. The police are a constant presence—talking into their radios, their heads swerving at all times, looking for anything off, wrong or inconsistent with how they expect things to run: orderly, smooth and stress-free.

I stop for a moment, distracted by several police officers running toward a lone bag sitting off near the end of the walkway outside the main entrance.

As I stare I feel a shove from behind, look back and find myself staring into the gridded mask of another officer.

"Move along," he says calmly, "now."

I head into Arthur Chin.

Arthur Chin is no longer an airport of the early part of the century, a place where families gathered with their bags and children and dogs and noise as they headed off on vacations to beaches and amusement parks and relatives' homes, and business men and women weaved in between them, suits sharp, bags small and packed tight, all efficiency, no fat, no noise, no fuss.

Now you go to the airport for three reasons.

If you are a member of a connected family—the 1-Percenters as they are now known, families with money and power, families who recognized that the country's debts would come due eventually and that it was better to shift allegiances east—then you still vacation.

1-Percenters charter private flights through China Southern Airlines to vacation spots primarily domestic, occasionally abroad, and always owned, secured and run by the Corporation. They are safe havens filled with sprawling hotels, entertainment and exotic foods—all things you know once existed in some sense for everyone. But not anymore because they are now only available, and only accessible, to those who work behind the scenes. These are the people pulling levers, moving money, making decisions, yet hidden away—there, but not; unseen, yet still affecting every moment of every day and every decision you make.

A small pack of armored soldiers run by me: a group of ten men and women perfectly synchronized in lock step, with arms pumping and machine guns bouncing on their backs with each step.

Soldiers are endlessly deployed from Arthur Chin to tamp down insurrections and uprisings by militia groups and nativists in places like Wyoming or Maine. Areas left for dead—abandoned to the remaining inhabitants, nature and time.

This is the second reason why someone might come to Arthur Chin. Arthur Chin is the central deployment hub for all things military—the Midwest now the dominant region of the country due to its isolation and location far away from oceans and the myriad things that cannot be wholly controlled by the Corporation.

After the soldiers pass, I see two or three other travelers like myself getting ready for travel to the stars: alone, no family, light bags, no guns or uniforms.

And this is the third reason someone comes to Arthur Chin—Arthur Chin is home to the remaining fleet of retired space shuttles. The space shuttles are no longer used for any practical scientific purpose, but instead are now used for the occasional space tourist, though more likely for salesmen like me, doing the work of the Corporation and trying to move property in far away worlds.

As I step into the terminal, the police watching the entrance put their hands in the air to remind me and the guy arriving at the same moment as me that we need to stop before entering any further. All the police wear black from head to toe, steel-toed boots and helmets with masks of intersecting carbon fiber grids that cover their faces like a sieve, filtering everything that comes in and out.

It doesn't matter that there hasn't been a bombing in decades. The fact is, if you want to blow up a city, few things still work better than a plane, and if you don't believe that, you just need to look at pictures of what New York City and Los Angeles looked like when they still existed. They were stunning.

"Please remove your clothes and walk forward slowly," a dull, flat voice says from above. "The brain scan will commence in approximately three seconds…"

Everyone arriving at Arthur Chin goes through a naked-body scan before being allowed to enter the main terminal. You run your clothes and bags through the X-ray machine while walking through a second funnel-shaped fluoroscope that checks not only for hidden objects but also for elevated activity of any kind in the Amygdala.

I have nothing to hide, and yet I feel my neck tighten and my stomach suddenly become a bundle of nerves, the exact reaction I need to avoid and neutralize. I look at the guy to my right, he is impassive and Zen, I need to be like him. I think about kite-surfing, hugging Joey, laying in Shalla's arms, playing the guitar. Anything that will help me relax.

Remain calm. Breathe. Good. Just not too good, you never want to be too good, or too calm, because too calm is also a red flag, a sign that you may be up to something. Breathe. Be cool. Smile. Just don't overdo it. They watch everything now, every twitch, every movement and gesture, searching for any discernable sign that you do not want to be watched.

A thousand hot little fingers begin to stroke, prod and search me for anything that might be hidden, and anything that might inflict damage. The fingers are at first external, and almost sensual in their absolute attention to my every inch, curve and crevasse. But soon, too soon really, the fingers move away from the surface and head internally, now tracing every bone, organ and blood vessel, moving up, down, across and throughout me, no longer sensual, now all about penetration and exposure of anything that may otherwise not want to be found.

I try to concentrate again on good things, ignoring the feeling of having my stomach, bladder, liver, heart and lungs pricked by thousands of little pins, and I can mostly ignore them, or at least bare them, until the scan concludes by passing through my retinas and into my brain.

It's all consuming.

Like having my head hugged from the inside, and hugged too hard, and too unexpectedly, everything being crushed, squeezed, bruised and rolled, breathing near impossible.

And then it's done. Just like that.

But I am not done with security, not officially. There is still the interview. Everyone has an interview before entering any aircraft of any kind.

I put my clothes back on and walk toward the interview room escorted by two of the E.C.s. The guy who was next to me starts to walk away as well, but then the police officer across from him puts his hand up, signaling him to stop moving. The guy continues on though, seemingly oblivious to the police officer and what is expected. Several police officers quickly emerge from all directions, wrestle him to the ground and begin dragging him away as he screams, "I'm not a terrorist. I'm just high on SynthKhat…"

The interview room is cool, streamlined—a table, two chairs, one window, what is clearly a two-way mirror, bright lights.

In the middle of the table is a simple box, comprised of a handful of knobs and a single cable with a clip on the end.

On the far side of the table already seated is a guy with smooth skin, a roundish baby face and short red hair. He's wearing a white dress shirt as wrinkle-free as his face—no tie, his coat neatly hanging from the back of his chair. He could be my age, he could be any age.

The two E.C.s go stand behind him, silent, unmoving, hands clasped behind their backs, and he stands up to greet me, with a half smile, but welcoming.

"Norrin Radd, welcome," the baby-faced guy says extending his hand to shake, "this will be painless, I promise."

It's here, now, that the Corporation looks to remind you who is in charge, who will always be in charge, and that as needed, or wanted, they can do whatever they want, whenever they want.

There's just one problem with that.

"What's up Morg," I say, "fancy meeting you here?"

"Its Steven," Morg says, "I left that nickname behind when I left BeiShan."

There was a time when Morg was also known as the Executioner, so nicknamed because of his near-compulsive ruthlessness, his desire to be the muscle in our pack and his complete inability to let even the most minor of slights pass without retribution.

Not that this was the whole picture.

Morg also always seemed like he was slumming, a junkie SynthKhat dilettante who came and went as he wanted to, and then one day was just gone. We assumed his rich parents had been supporting him during this phase and that when they were done doing so, so was he. Sitting here it looks like we were right. Morg is exactly where children of connected parents end up, working for the Corporation. And the fact that he is working as an enforcer only reinforces the idea that you can put someone in a suit and clean them up, but it doesn't change who they are inside. People are who they are, and they rarely surprise you if you're paying attention.

All of which might be entertaining, except that there's a catch, and yes, there is always a catch isn't there?

When I wanted Shalla to have the baby, I needed money to make it happen. There were doctors, the delivery room, all of it. I went to Al B. He went to Morg. And here we are.

"Sorry, Steven," I say, "what a nice surprise."

"I bet it is," Morg says. "Of course you know all about surprises, right? So, how does it feel to be the newest member of the Joyful Future Real Estate sales team? It's exciting, right?"

"Yes, it is, very exciting, and a little scary…"

"I'm sure it is," Morg says. "So hey, as we get started here, could you put that clip at the end of the cable in front of you on your right index finger? Thanks. We use that to measure the Galvanic Skin response. It lets us know what's going on with you. Not that I'm saying anything is going on. Is there anything going on?"

"No bro, nothing going on here," I reply as I reach out to the cable and finger the clip for a moment before attaching it. On contact, the box the cable is attached to starts to vibrate slightly, almost purring.

"Anyway Norrin, the new job is a little scary, anything else?" Morg asks.

"I feel very conflicted about being away from family…"

"I bet you do. How is Shalla doing?" Morg says, acting like he doesn't know everything already. "It's been a long time. And Joey, right, how's he?"

"They're good, great. I'm very lucky and all of this is for them. But leaving them, and leaving them for so long, not seeing them, not being there for them, I feel a little sick about that. Especially since I'm also excited about it, the adventure, traveling the stars, it's very hard," I say.

"Of course it is, and you will say hello for me when you see her next, won't you?" Morg says, winking at me.

"Yes, sure, she'll be happy to hear I saw you," I say lying as politely as I can.

"Right, bullshit, whatever," Morg continues, "now what about Lebowski?"

"What do you mean?" I say.

"What do you talk about?" Morg asks.

"The waves, work, the waves," I say. "Not much, I don't really know him all that well."

"Okay," Morg replies, "and what about your mother,

Elmar. She killed herself didn't she?"

I think about my mother, her long hair, singing to me, baking cakes, all so long ago.

"She did," I say, "and she didn't leave a note or anything."

"And you found her?" Morg asks.

"I did, there was no one else who could have. It was just the two of us. You know all this Morg. Is this necessary?" I say getting upset and noticing the box my finger is attached to start to shake slightly.

"It's Steven," Morg says his voice rising slightly. "Moving on, your father, Jartan, left you when you were very young. That must have been hard?"

"I don't know. My mom did what she could for as long as she could," I say. "He was never really there, and I never really knew any differently."

Morg leans forward across the table, turns one of the knobs on the box I'm attached to, before interlocking his fingers and trying to look empathic, or maybe it's serious, I can't get a fix on him.

"Do you think the Corporation made your father disappear Norrin?" Morg says. "And look man, there's no wrong answer. This is important, but there's no wrong answer, really."

"There were rumors, and my mom made some allusions to that possibility," I say noticing a slight hum cascading across my index finger to the clip and back again, "but I don't know, and I don't care. I want to be a good father, and that takes up enough of my energy."

The box vibrates again and Morg takes a brief sidelong glance at it. He then leans back into his chair.

"Seriously," I say, "do you want me to pretend that I don't know that you already know all of this?"

"Whatever works for you," Morg says.

"Okay, cool, I will do what I need to do," I say.

"I know you will," Morg says standing up, extending his hand to shake and waving off the E.C.s still standing there silently.

When it is just the two of us, Morg walks over to my side of the table and leans forward like he plans to whisper something in my ear.

"Let's talk debt Norrin, you owe me a lot of money," Morg says. "This job will help, but now that you have it, you're going to need to show a lot more initiative. Wouldn't you agree?"

"I guess," I say, "but what does that mean?"

"That means that you are going to do me a favor," Morg says. "There will be a box waiting for you on the shuttle just before you land, and you will deliver it to a location in Happiness Sector, no questions asked. Got it? Good."

"And then we're square?" I ask.

"I wouldn't say square," Morg replies, "let's call it getting there."

"Fine dude, whatever you say, anything else?" I say.

"No that's it for now; get out of here and enjoy your adventure," Morg says, "well after you stop in the Terrax lab of course."

14

The Terrax lab is all white, spotless and glowing; a soft hum of purity and cleanliness washing over the room. There is a hospital bed off to one side of the room, an array of computers and padded walls. Lights blast forth from everywhere and every possible angle, exposing and crippling everything and anything in its path. The rush of light is so piercing that I am blinded as I walk in and shocked after my eyes adjust to see someone standing before me in a doctor's coat.

At first he is an amorphous blob, an undulating mass of whiteness, blurry and unfocused. But slowly he becomes himself—wan, long-haired and thin, yet stony looking, square faced, his jaw as massive as a shovel.

"What we think we know about Terraxes," says the man in the doctor's coat stentorianly, "should not be confused with what the actual truth may be. Terraxes are identical to us in every way and in fact believe they are us. Which is important, because they need to make the decisions we would make, know what we know, and create a sense of reality that retains the whiff of dream, even as time passes and their job is done. It is a blending between what they are and who you are, and even if your spouse will later have moments where they recall hazy memories about their time together, a kind of déjà vu if you will, that is less about what was, and all about the near seamlessness of the transition from you to Terrax to you again."

Is there a correct response to that? I can't think of one so I settle for, "hello."

"Hello, I'm Dr. Thanos," the stony-looking dude says smiling, "and now that I've shared my philosophical views on Terraxes we can proceed. This will be painless, promise."

"Can I hold you to that," I say trying to crack a joke.

Dr. Thanos pauses, looks up to the corner of the room at a camera and then looks back at me again.

"Not legally," he says, no longer smiling.

Now it is my turn to pause. I look at the camera as well, wondering who is watching us, Morg maybe, definitely, and who else, who knows.

"Gotcha," Dr. Thanos says smiling again, but maybe a little sinister now as well. "Do you think you're the only one who can joke around here? C'mon, we're all friends and we're all on the same team. In fact, call me by my first name, Beck, if you want, no don't, joking. Or am I? Anyway, sit up on the bed then, alright? Alright, let's get down to business."

"Sure," I say unconvinced and hopping up and onto the bed.

"You know Norrin, in the early years of the Terrax program there were problems," says Dr. Thanos, pausing to move the hair out of his face. "The Terraxes didn't want to leave their jobs, and why would they—they think they are you, and your family is theirs; they believe they are where they are supposed to be. There was confusion, late night raids and the occasional hostage situation, some bloodshed and disappearances. But we fixed this by embedding a chip in the Terraxes' brains, a psychic on-off switch. The chip is initiated upon your departure and begins to wind down on the approximate day of your return. By the time you get home, they are no longer you, and then we assign them the odd jobs that no one else is willing to do. As the Terraxes age and eventually wear down, the chip turns off, and their parts are recycled for transplants and other physical improvements needed by the 1-Percenters and Corporation leaders. Not bad, right?"

"I guess not," I say thinking about the outer stretches of Baidu, the chaos and fear, the lack of work, and how little Dr. Thanos probably cares about any of that.

"Alright then, we will begin by taking a DNA sample from the inside of you cheek," Dr. Thanos says, reaching into his pocket and removing a long metallic cotton swab.

He rotates the swab in my mouth, the taste of metal lingering for a moment on the back of my tongue. I am reminded of the DNA test I took when Shalla was first pregnant with Joey.

"Painless, right?" Dr. Thanos says.

"Mostly," I say, "though the taste of metal is as unpleasant as the memories it brings up."

"Ah, your son," Dr. Thanos, "that turned out okay though, right?"

I start to ask him how he knows about Joey and Al B and the confusion around all of that. But it's pointless, and not just because he can't say anything. They know everything, everything, and accepting that is easier than constantly acting like you're surprised by it.

"It turned out great," I say, thinking about the nape of Joey's neck and how his chest flutters up and down as he sleeps, one arm always thrown across his face. I start to cry, which startles me, though not half as much as when Dr. Thanos collects several of the tears in a vial.

"Fantastic," Dr. Thanos says, "every little bit helps, now lay back if you wouldn't mind so I can gather some more material."

I put my head on the pillow and watch as Dr. Thanos goes about his work. First he deftly plucks out a small chunk of hair by the roots and then lightly scrapes some skin off of my arms, legs and face, placing all of the materials in separate vials.

"Okay, Norrin, just one more step," Dr. Thanos says more seriously, "we need some of your memories so that we can fully realize your Terrax brain."

"How do you that," I say, not really wanting an answer to this question.

"Don't be scared," Dr. Thanos says, "I am going to give you a shot: you will briefly lose your memory and during that time we will use an MRI to scrub your cerebrum and search for the basic building blocks of memory—birth, childhood, happy things, upsetting things. Whatever serves as a trigger for you we want to capture it and duplicate it, but don't worry, it's harmless and you won't remember the experience at all."

"What if I don't remember anything when I awake," I ask, "and then never remember anything again. Does that ever happen?"

"Not anymore," Dr. Thanos replies smiling again. "When you awake you will immediately head to your shuttle, memory intact, marvelous adventures to follow."

"Will I get to see my Terrax?" I ask.

Dr. Thanos stiffens at that. His reaction is subtle and quick, but it happens before he regains his composure and forces a smile.

"It's not against the rules, but we don't recommend it," Dr. Thanos says, "too much potential confusion for you. Got it?"

I don't got anything, but I'm sure Dr. Thanos and whoever he reports to would prefer that I wasn't curious about any of this.

"I don't think so," I say, "why would it be confusing for me?"

"Imagine meeting your better self, your best self," Dr. Thanos replies, closing his eyes for a moment, and briefly lost in thought. "Imagine looking into the eyes of the you that has no regrets, doesn't suffer from irrational fears or jealousy, a mirror image that really isn't in your real image at all."

"Who would even want that," I say, "it's not human."

"True," says Dr. Thanos, "but as humans we have no idea what we want before it's before us. Think about Joey—you had no idea how much you wanted to be a parent until you were, and you certainly had no idea that you could love something so much that you could kill for it, or worse, leave it if you had to, so as to make its life better, right?"

There is no response to any of this, but I do know that I never have known what I wanted, not really, and that everything up to this point has just sort of happened.

"Alright, I'm good," I say, "no more questions."

"Good, then close your eyes and begin counting back from ten," Dr. Thanos says, inserting an IV into my forearm, the contact dye flowing into my veins, my body beginning to glow—the last image I see.

15

I am wandering down the tunnel that leads me from the Terrax lab to the terminal where my shuttle awaits. Multicolored lights are firing at me from every direction, and I turn my head with each light, looking here, no here, there, and there, and here again, the sidewalk is moving below me, always moving forward, and taking me toward some kind of destiny.

I am Norrin Radd.

This realization hits me like it had never occurred to me before, though more accurately it hits me like I had sort of forgotten it even as I thought only moments before that I knew exactly who I was.

Didn't I?

But of course that's the trick with memory, you always think you know exactly what you need to know until confronted with the fact that you do not.

I am married to Shalla.

I have a son named Joey.

I, I, I....

My memory is coming back. First leaking in, in dribs and drabs, and then in rivulets that begin to grow into a flood of thoughts, feelings, events, pains, joy and glories.

I am Norrin Radd and I am walking through the bowels of Arthur Chin. I live in Baidu and I am heading into space today, now, when I get to the end of this sidewalk.

I kite-surf, I play guitar, my mom used to bake me cakes, and my dad disappeared.

I'm running, I don't know why I'm running, it's as if I need to escape the rush of memories now pounding into me like a wave.

I love the Ramones; the touch of Shalla's hair, fingers, stomach, thighs and breasts; Joey raising his arms up toward me for a hug; the smell of fall and rain.

No, wait, maybe this is not escape but something else— maybe I'm running toward the memories and letting them wash over me like a shower, fresh and intoxicating, and full of rebirth.

Maybe.

And now I am smiling, but out of breath and leaning against the window at my gate. The shuttle looms there outside the window, like something from another world, a bird or a dream: something, though, something magnificent.

16

"Just lie back, relax, we are preparing to leave," a calming voice says—it's not metallic or robotic, not scratchy or booming, it's not meant to offend or dominate. It's there to soothe, to remind you that there is goodness and comfort in this world, if not the next, and you need to believe it, embrace it and never forget that this voice is there for you and only you regardless of the truth. For what's truth anyway—just something you accept as fact, regardless of what might be the case.

I lie back and an E.C. enters the room to give me a sedative so that I will fall asleep for the start of our journey.

"You will soon be asleep," the voice continues, making love to me and wrapping me in warmth and joy.

Sedatives are wonderful, but this is about more than sleep, it's also about nourishment and replenishment, and drugs alone can't guarantee that, hence the voice.

The voice is female, the voice of the lover, the wife, the object of desire, affection and need, and ultimately the mother, everyone's mother who ever lived. The first voice you hear upon entering the world, a time when everything is possible, when love is pure, and when the possibility of endless fear and confusion is still muted and tamped down, because at that moment, and this moment, it doesn't have to be that way.

"Close your eyes. Think good things, happy things," the voice says.

Not everyone can make it through this moment: the moment of departure, the moment just before space beckons. For some the anxiety is too great, the fear of the unknown too overwhelming. And while they could give us drugs that halt our memory as they do in the Terrax lab, no one can spend months in space travel with no memories of take-off to draw from.

Without memories there would be no dreams, and without dreams we would slowly die, cell by cell, moment by moment, something the Corporation only learned after failing to understand this before they began sending people so far away.

"You're doing great, just take a deep breath," the voice says as the engines on the shuttle come to life with an enormous hiccup of electricity and fire and life, the slight scent of ethanol wafting past me as I settle back even further into my bed.

I take a deep breath and then another, my eyelids growing heavy and crashing together. There is movement below me and around me, a slight hum, some grinding, and there is life. There is also the sense of being pushed from below and above all at once, compressed between invisible hands, flattened and stretched.

Breathe. Think good things, surfing, making love, chewing SynthKhat on the beach, holding Joey.

And now there is floating, floating and spinning and spinning and floating, weightless and fatigued, so very fatigued.

17

I am running home from school, the leaves at my feet rustle and launch into the air before spinning back to the ground by the blades of the black helicopters flying overhead and circling the neighborhood like enormous metal vultures—watching, always watching, but not doing anything more, nothing obvious anyway.

They don't matter though. They have nothing to do with me, or school, or getting home to see my mom, who is waiting for me. Looking out the window as a cake cooks somewhere in the background. Its vanilla scent saturating the kitchen, the house, the block and my mom, who always smells like baked goods, all sweet and warm and safe. Not that I know what that means. It just is something I am, not something I need to be or figure out, or wonder what it means to get there and how to do so.

There she is, standing, smiling and waiting by the curtain. Her red hair twisted behind her neck, her hands at her waist interlocked. Her fingers always moving, wringing, intersecting, twisting. I'm willing her to stand still, smile, and be there. Like a rock. My rock. My dad somewhere, maybe coming home, maybe not, but knowing it doesn't matter, that it's okay because she is there.

I rush into the kitchen and I am knocked over as always by the smell of the vanilla, the subtle presence of chocolate, the sugary goodness of frosting and a touch of molasses; no, honey; no, both; no, I'm not sure what. But it's there, and we are sitting at the table now, eating cake, smiling, talking about school, and girls, and music, and then there is a sound behind me. A foot step, a breath.

Someone wanting to be quiet, so close, but not quite able to be.

For a moment my mother's hands stop moving, and the smile becomes half, still happy but something else as well, something more equivocal. Is that worry, pain, confusion, all of it? Maybe, yes, no, don't know, she's not moving, just paused, and so I turn around and it's my dad emerging from the shadows, engulfing me in his enormous arms and burying his clean-shaven head in my neck, taking in my smell and warmth before moving to my mom, now engulfing her as well, grabbing a chunk of cake with his hand and lifting my mom into the air.

They are laughing and the room is filled with joy and awe, and then they are drifting upstairs. I am left in the kitchen with the cake and the setting sun and the occasional helicopter buzzing ever closer to the house, but not quite stopping, never stopping, just looming, dipping and swaying in a dance of its own making.

Why am I asleep at the kitchen table? Where are my mom and dad? When did it become so dark and cold? What is all that noise? Is that the swoosh of helicopter blades, the heavy sounds of boots slapping the ground, the click of guns, the pounding of fists on the door? Knocking, then pummeling, followed by the rush of soldiers. No faces, guns up, breathing heavy, sweat in the air, a full rush into the house, and through the kitchen before heading up the stairs where my parents, are, went, must be.

I chase them, these monsters in the night, invaders, terrorists all, whether they work for the Corporation or God, or wherever they come from, hurtling forth from the darkness. Now they, we, are in my parent's room. They are naked and flush, hair and skin, everywhere. My dad is trying to get to the window, but they have him, and they are dragging him out of his room and down the stairs and through the kitchen. He's smiling, and nodding his head, and he's gone, so gone, and it's just us now, and I am the man of the house, now and forever.

18

I jolt awake, puffy and weak, my eyes bulging from my head like an anime character in a book that Joey might read.

Where am I?

I am here, of course, somewhere, yes, here, somewhere.

But where, is this BeiShan, Shalla's arms, the kitchen, my mom, what, what is this? I am shaking, no shivering, I don't know. I know I cannot breathe though. I cannot calm down. I try get up, but I cannot move. My legs are jelly. My arms don't work. Nothing is responding, nothing, nothing works any more. My mouth is so dry. I could drink forever, anything, now, now please, what, where am I? I am not with Shalla, this is not Baidu or my kitchen or anything at all.

Fuuuuuuuuuuuuuuck!

Lights are coming on. The glare burns my bulging eyes, my skin, my brain. I put my hand up in front of my face, shielding myself from that which I do not know.

"Relax, breathe," the calming voice says, the voice of reason, love and the mother, always the mother.

She's back, and I can relax.

I breathe.

"Slowly move your hands and feet," the voice continues, "you are alright."

How does she know this?

Because she knows everything, she must, I trust that, and know it to be unequivocally true. It has to be so. I shake my hands and feet, at first just moving millimeters at a time, and then something more, bending, and blood flow, and my eyes begin to adjust, my brain no longer so fried, my skin beginning to cool.

"It is time to awaken," the voice says, mellifluously, the room coated in honey, well, honey and love, "please stand up, slowly."

I tell my legs to stand, to swing over the side of the bed, but they do not. I grasp the sides of the bed and lift myself up to a sitting position, blood immediately rushing to my head, brain pounding and eyes itching and pulsing and ready to leap from my skull.

I rub my forehead until the moment passes and then inch by inch I shift my legs to the side of the bed, before lifting my right foot, then my left, over the side, leaving them dangling for what looks like miles above the floor.

I push off of the bed and feel a jolt ripple through my legs, starting with my feet, before moving through my calves, knees, thighs and into my hips.

I pee in my pants.

But I'm standing. I'm good. As good as I can be.

"Please proceed to the shower station just outside the door," the voice says.

I am embarrassed at how erect I am, how quickly and achingly, thinking of Shalla and my mom, the voice, and any woman I have ever met and thought I might have had a shot at.

"After your shower, please exit the door and follow the hall until you reach the cafeteria," the voice continues, and for a moment I believe the voice will follow me into the shower and finish off this phase of the trip with a happy ending.

I enter the shower station and begin to stroke my cock even as hot water starts to cascade across my willing skin for the first time, in how long, and how many miles—too many, and a whole world ago at that.

19

I exit the shower station: clean, shaven, primped and suited-up. I walk down the hall as directed and as I turn into the cafeteria, I hear a familiar voice.

"Hello sir, welcome back to the world of living."

I am facing an E.C., not mine, but one so similar to mine I feel a sudden and rippling attack of loss and isolation and sadness and all the things that make being homesick so real and vibrant.

As I look away in embarrassment and across the cafeteria—all sleek, steely smoothness and harsh light—I see Ricky and two guys I don't know sitting around a table drinking coffee.

"How fucking beautiful is that," Ricky says as he jumps up to hug me, "the kid is back and ready to do some damage, right kid?"

His hair and teeth are as perfect as ever, which makes me feel better, more like home, some version of home anyway.

"Hey kid," Ricky says, "today, now, is lesson one on the journey, alright, okay, great."

"Right now," I say, brain cells still activating.

"Right now baby," Ricky says, "no time like the present. And to help us out are the Geology boys, Dave and George."

"Geologists?" I ask looking over at Dave and George, both of whom sport close-cropped haircuts, interesting choices in facial hair and dark sunglasses.

"That's what they tell me," Ricky says. "It's all mineral rights and exotic metals up there; real estate is the just the half off it. It's the wild fucking west up there kid and don't let anyone tell you any differently."

"Word," George says, his mouth buried somewhere underneath a massive beard.

"Fu is currently the only operating, hospitable urban center on Mars," Dave says, constantly twisting the ends of a gnarly Fu Manchu mustache between his fingers. "It's a temporary city covered by an enormous dome as high as Burj Khalifa and composed of boron carbide and Teflon…"

"Temperature is controlled," George says, cutting Dave off. "Oxygen is managed, no dust or invaders welcome."

"None, welcome," Dave repeats and then turns to George for a high five.

I start to think that Dave and George might be something other than Geologists.

"Anyway," Ricky says joining in, "Fu is divided into five sectors…"

"And what does Fu mean?" I ask.

"Good fortune," Ricky says. "So, there are five sectors. The first is Prosperity Sector, which is filled with an endless series of offices and factories representing the companies given permission to build there. That is where our office is, which is, how should I put it, quaint."

"There's also the Good Luck and Happiness Sectors," George says, "which are composed of entertainment and housing for people who are working on Mars on an extended basis. Good Luck has movies, restaurants and shopping."

"And Happiness is filled with massage parlors, night clubs, bars and other creature comforts for those long away from home," Dave says.

"Not that you care about that, right kid?" Ricky says winking.

"No I don't, I'm happily married," I reply maybe a little too stridently as both Dave and George laugh to themselves.

"Family man, love that," Ricky says. "Okay, the Wealth Sector is set aside for visiting government officials and the 1-Percenters looking at the real estate and imagining their future homes and lives. This is where we will go for our sales calls. Got it?"

"Got it," I say, "and what's the fifth sector?"

"Longevity Sector houses the military, and you will definitely have no reason to go there," George says no longer laughing.

"None, really?, c'mon," I say smiling and trying to break the newfound tension in the room.

"No, none," Dave says, "it's for your safety. Cool?"

"Sure, but why do we even need the military there," I say, knowing how ridiculous that must sound to them.

Dave and George both visibly stiffen, jaws tight, lips pursed.

"This is a peaceful mission," George says, "so let's just say the military is there as peacekeepers."

"Works for me," I say.

"I think that's enough for now kid," Ricky says looking at Dave and George. "Next time we talk sales."

20

I climb back into my chair and recline, no need for the voice tonight. I am exhausted and crazy for more sleep.

Now.

There.

I am running home, the scent of vanilla filling my brain. I want my mother and that sense of safety, goodness and nurturing. I want it so much. I don't want to be the man all the time. I want to be held and soothed and comforted. But she is not in the window, and there are no cakes or scents, just silence and stillness, coldness and vastness, loss, a lack of everything that it means to be alive. Nothing is on. Nothing is moving or whirring or breathing. No sound, no vibrations, but for the low hum of the helicopter blades that are always present.

I run into the kitchen as the soldiers once did, and up the stairs, but she is not here or there. The bathroom door is half-open though, a splash of light, and there, there are her hands, and her red hair wet from the bath water. She is naked, the porcelain skin, submerged, floating, sinking, receding, melting into the calm of the water. Her blood is splashed across the bathtub wall, and her life has slowly passed from this world to the next one drip at a time. I am holding her, but it is too late, there is no life and no safety, and then I am gone, running again until I find myself on BeiShan.

There is Morg, Al B and his girlfriend, lover, muse Shalla, and her flowing hair and raucous, throaty laugh. They hustle and make music, rhyming and stealing. They play at Berlin, a club on BeiShan, chew on SynthKhat, and fuck, lolling about, squatting here, there and everywhere, dodging the black helicopters and spinning from this to that and this.

They embrace me, and they take me off of the street and into their arms, their band, and their bed. We are good and happy and Al B's the leader, but Shalla needs something else, needs someone else, and I know how to be needed. I am need, and she is pregnant, and who, what, how, when? Who knows? Al B is gone, Morg is gone, because people are always gone, going, gone, and there are the two of us, and there is Joey, and here, no there, no here we are.

21

Awake again.

But today I know who I am. The blood is flowing. The legs are strong. The brain is alert. I make my way to the cafeteria, where Ricky awaits me, coffee in hand, hair perfect, smile in place.

"Ready Freddy?" Ricky asks.

"Sure," I say, "and what, no Dave and George today?"

"Not today," Ricky says, "they don't do sales—minerals, some security, that's their thing, but this here, now, this is my thing and soon enough your thing as well. Cool?"

"Cool," I say, "let's do this.

"Great," Ricky says, "come with me to the training room."

We walk down one sleek hall to the next until we reach one of a series of nondescript doors.

Ricky pauses.

"What we're going to do here is a role play," Ricky says "There is a couple in the room and they will play the part of the prospective buyers. They are 1-Percenters who are ready to leave Earth, but not quite. They know it's time to move on and they know there is money to be made here. But it involves leaving all they've ever known and so we have to make it feel to them like this is exactly what they want and need."

"Don't people want to leave?" I ask.

"Sure they do," Ricky says, "but fear will always override want and common sense."

"Okay," I say tentatively, "I can do this."

"Yes you can," Ricky says, "and you'll be great. I know it. And here's how it will go down—I will start, and when you feel comfortable, just jump in, alright?"

"Jump, got it," I say, "and hey, where did the couple come from?"

"They're Terraxes—their jobs back at home were done. They will help us here, and when we get to Fu they'll do manual labor or be harvested for parts. Circle of Life babe," Ricky says.

"It's funny how often people say that," I say as we walk in.

"What?" Ricky says, easing into the zone.

"Nothing bro," I say, "Hakuna Mattata."

The room is sparsely furnished. There is a sturdy look-ing table where the Terraxes are already sitting in chairs, and nothing else especially extraordinary except for the fake window on the wall which is fakely overlooking the sweeping and still underdeveloped red deserts of Mars.

"This is about innovation," Ricky says as we settle into the chairs across from the Terraxes, and I know from my previous training that we always start with that, because people want to feel like they're part of something new and exciting.

The goal is to conjure up the idea of what might be. Every situation is different, every family, with different needs, wants and desires, but ultimately you are selling dreams and hope, a fantasy world that does not quite yet exist, but will.

"Why would we want to do this," the male Terrax asks, his light skin and grey eyes just short of humming with any real vitality.

"Why," Ricky says, "let me tell you why. Mars is not only a place that you will be able to raise your children, and their children, and generations to come, but it's a whole new world where anything is possible, because we are building it together, a wondrous vision full of green living and unending promise."

"Why can't we just rebuild Earth, I love Baidu," the female Terrax says, her red corkscrew curls nearly on fire as they cascade across her fiercely freckled cheeks.

"Because you deserve the best," I say a little too enthusiastically as I jump in, "because you are unique, and so is Mars."

I stop for a moment to catch my breath and calm myself.

"And this, this is an opportunity to be part of the kind of world you deserve to be part of," I add because I want them to feel that they are special.

"Can I be frank?" Ricky says leaning forward.

"Of course," the male Terrax says placing his arm around the female Terrax's shoulders.

"This will be a world where you only have to interact with people like you. Beautiful and smart and proper, raised right, from good families, families that have built things too and given of themselves, in war, commerce, and philanthropy. Your families had a different idea for earth that just didn't work out. There was too much debt. The world governments couldn't reign in the extremists or track all the nuclear warheads being trafficked here. The poor began to rebel, and the streets, waterways and even the sky became places you could only visit with trepidation," Ricky says practically whispering the last lines.

The Terraxes may be role-playing, but they are hanging on every word.

"And you are accustomed to something different," I say, "raised to think things would always be different and better for you."

I tell them this, because they believe it, they have been insulated, or should be from the world they never understood, the one outside of what they know. What we know, and what they know, is that their world is now all about enclaves and armed guards, and threat, to their way of life, and legacy.

"Earth is no longer a world where you can be yourselves and celebrate all you've done and earned over the many years your families were building something better, more stable, and more lasting. We all want roots and identity, social norms we understand, not to mention culture, art, beauty and love, friends and networks, kinship and a life worth living to its fullest. And you can have that, here, now, soon," I go on to say, "but you have to take a chance, and you have to leave what you know behind."

What we know is that they know they can't hold on much longer. Not really. Not when everything is slowly disintegrating except for that which they control, and that which they control becomes smaller and smaller every day, year and generation, from this millennia into the next.

"The thing is, Ricky says, "what if you don't get here before things truly implode? Well, then there may be no getting here at all."

The Terraxes are now wholly absorbed, ripe for the picking and Ricky is just reeling them in.

"Unlike Earth," I say, "we can get it right here—no war, no global warming, or famine, no terror or extremists or fear. It will just be us, well you, and your families, celebrating a way of life you have earned, and what could be better than that? Nothing, nothing is better than that and it is what you deserve. So here's your chance to grab it, and you do want to grab it, don't you? Yes, yes, you do, and for so little down, come on, there you go."

Ultimately, it's not just hope we're selling, but hope disguised and built on fear, fear of a lost way of life that can be regained here, and so easily, but it must be soon, now, because the space will go fast, and if they lose their spot here, where will they go?

Nowhere and we all know that.

"Don't forget, it's not like we're going to Venus yet," Ricky says, "or Neptune, not for a long time, maybe ever, and the Moon experiment didn't work out. So what will you have, just the earth and its slow freefall to nothing; savageness, lack of civility, violence and nothing, nothing but fear anyway."

"We'll sign," the Terraxes say together mesmerized and smiling.

And then we all shake hands. We laugh and hug. And Ricky slaps me on the back.

22

Ricky and I are receiving massages from a pair of female E.C.s. We are on our backs, undressed, sheets at our waists. It is the night before we arrive on Mars. We are supposed to be preparing for battle, but I am stuck on being so far from home and what it means to be okay with that.

"Look kid," Ricky says, "it's what we do, we're salesman, and salesman sell, let it go."

"But you have kids right and a wife, can you really justify being away and not caring for them, by saying that you're a salesman and that's what you do, done, that's all?" I respond, "I'm not sure I can do that."

"You have to separate yourself from that and them," Ricky says. "It's two different lives, two different buckets. I lose myself in the work and I don't think about it. There can be no thinking. Period. And you can't think about it either."

"But then how are you any different that an E.C.—no offense," I say looking up at the E.C., who just nods as she works on my shoulders, then arms, "or your Terrax? Is that being human?"

"It's coping kid," Ricky says, "it's how we get by."

"And what about the Terraxes," I continue, "how do you deal with one living in your home as you, doesn't it drive you crazy?"

"Like Shelley," Ricky says chuckling, "sorry, I didn't say that out loud, but same thing, Norrin; I don't think about it. I can't think about it. I am work. Be work kid."

"I'm not sure I can be that guy," I say.

"We'll see," Ricky replies, "if you can't, you're Shelley; if you're you can, you're me, time will tell."

Is that really all there is? I think as the E.C. starts kneading my forearms and palms, my body going limp. Are there really no other options?

I look over at Ricky, he looks relaxed, content.

"Is that it," I blurt out, "are those really the only options?"

"It is if you want to work," Ricky says, "and if you're going to be like me, you better learn how to take care of yourself."

"What does that mean?" I say leaning-up on one elbow.

"She knows," Ricky says, looking dreamily at the E.C.

The E.C. slides her hand under Ricky's sheet, and I lie back down, eyes closed. I try to ignore thoughts of responsibility and Terraxes, and instead try to focus on good things—the surf and memories of my mom. I don't fully calm down, but I do begin to relax a little as the E.C. moves to my thighs and feet.

23

There is no sleep after the massage. And there won't be, so I head into the Simulator Room, put on a motion capture suit and goggles, and step in front of the green screen.

A small robotic belch emerges from above me.

"What shall we do today sir," the E.C. says, "do you want to fly across the cosmos or swim in the deepest seas?"

"I would like to kite-surf," I say, "across the Martian desert. Can that be arranged?"

"Of course sir, one moment," the E.C. replies.

It is quiet for a moment, but then there is wind in my face, harsh wind, biting and granular, the sand blasting into my cheeks, and an unexpectedly stifling heat baking my forehead.

Soon I am holding my kite, my feet flat on my board, shifting with the sand's constant undulations. The wind is coming from a variety of directions. I am gliding up and down the dunes, crossing valleys of all heights and depths, cutting through the sand like a knife and bouncing across the random streams of salt water carving errant crevasses across my path.

I am free. I am greatness. I am suddenly at the bottom of steep dune.

I start to climb, my calves and forearms aching, the sand biting my face, the sky as purple as a bruised plum. I begin to crest the top of the dune, and as I reach the peak I find myself hurtling into space, soaring and beautiful, a cosmic explorer, tiny and glowing, just another star to anyone on Earth.

I close my eyes and I take a deep breath. When I open them again I am standing alone in the Simulator Room alone with the green screen and the motion capture suit.

"What happened?" I say in barely a whisper.

"We will be arriving shortly, Mr. Radd," a voice says, burping to life somewhere above me "Please gather your belongings and buckle-up for the final descent."

24

There is a push and a rush and a slight metallic crunch. We are landing. I reach for my bag and there is a box. The box is small, rectangular, slightly glowing with a nearly, but not completely, imperceptible hum. Where did it come from? Morg, of course. There are debts to be paid. How did it get here? And does that even matter? I pick it up and watch it glow for a moment in my hands.

There is a metallic belch.

"Mr. Radd," the E.C. says, "you will deliver the box to the Good Luck Sector bazaar when the opportunity presents itself."

"Okay," I say, "and how will I know where to go?"

"The box will lead you, sir," the E.C. replies.

"What?" I say.

But there is a click, and then there is silence, though only for a moment.

"Hey kid," Ricky says walking in and hugging me, "it's show time, let's hit it."

We leave the shuttle and walk through the small airport that sits on the outskirts of Fu. Near the exit doors stands a male E.C. holding a sign that reads "Joyful Future Real Estate welcomes you."

"Hey there," Ricky says waving to the E.C., "we're the guys you're looking for."

"Welcome," the E.C. says, "please follow me."

As we walk out I see Dave and George decked out in what looks like military gear lifting several large bags and exiting a side door.

"Are you sure Dave and George are Geologists?" I say to Ricky as we climb into a waiting car.

"That's what they keep telling me," Ricky says, "and whatever they say is good enough for me."

We pass through the streets of Fu with a smoothness that belies the still mostly undeveloped nature of the streets and areas that fall outside of the four main sectors of the city. The top of the dome is nearly too high to see, but coming in from the airport you can see clearly what exists outside of the dome, sand dunes and wind, minimal vegetation and endless space to develop—first buildings, then neighborhoods, one day towns, urban centers and states. People will live here and they will thrive. Somewhere, someone has it all mapped out, and all we need to do is fill the vision with actual people.

"We are entering Prosperity Sector," the E.C. says.

The sparse urban space gives way to clusters of nondescript, low-hanging office buildings. Here there is an uptick of activity, actual sidewalks and people walking on them. And it's not like Baidu, not at first blush certainly. People actually stop and talk, and seemingly without fear of helicopters, guns or the unemployed assailing them. Nor are the homeless herded anywhere, because there don't seem to be any homeless either. I start to wonder what it would be like to bring Shalla and Joey here—a fresh start for us, full of possibility?—but I quickly kill that thought. This new world is for those of privilege and connection. We will never be welcomed here. Baidu is the end of the line for people like us.

"We're here," the E.C. says.

"Let's rock and roll," Ricky says.

Ricky and I enter one of the buildings that is otherwise no different from the one to the right or left except for the sign by the front door, which reads Joyful Future Real Estate.

There are no scanners here. You see a door and then you open it. We walk through the lobby and get to the front desk where we are met by a receptionist with long, black hair and blue-tinged skin.

"Hey there Ricky," she says, "how's it hanging?"

"Professional as always baby, love that," Ricky says, smiling before leaning way in toward the receptionist, moving her hair, placing his mouth next to her ear and talking low, though not so low that I can't hear him. "And it's hanging low, the toilet water was freezing this morning. Then again, you already know that, don't you?"

"Funny guy," the receptionist says playfully pushing Ricky away. "Tell me, who's your handsome friend? Is that your son? Is this like bring-your-kid-to-work day? I so didn't get that memo."

"Look who's the comedian now," Ricky says, "you ought to take your act on the road. You'd kill. And this is Norrin, he's the new guy. I'd tell you to go easy on him later when you break him in, but I might need a tune-up. It's been a long trip."

"And look who's professional now, nice and classy, as always," the receptionist says. "Welcome Norrin, your cubes are waiting."

"Thanks," I say as the door behind the desk opens.

"Later baby," Ricky says as we walk in.

"You know where to find me," she replies.

We walk into the sprawling office, rows and rows of cubes, and endless streams of people and the E.C.s zipping about the room.

I have all sorts of questions for Ricky, but only one to start with.

"Blue skin," I say quizzically, "what's it like hitting that?"

"She's cyanotic," Ricky says, "it's due to the oxygen deprivation from living here inside the dome for so long. And what's it like? They're all pink inside kid."

25

Ricky and I are standing in a demo house in Wealth Sector. The floor-to-ceiling windows are flush against the wall of the dome. An E.C. has prepared drinks and laid out crudités and little sandwiches. The couple sitting on the couch before us is young and refined, the wife sporting a still small but obvious pregnancy bump that juts out just slightly from her white oxford shirt. Her butterscotch skin reminds me of Shalla, but I ignore that and focus on the work before us.

We have been meeting with potential buyers for days, moving from one pair to the next. None can believe they are here, much less considering leaving home for this, an undeveloped planet of swirling sand and endless space. They can't picture what living here could mean, what they have is fear transforming into possibility and then back into fear again. Fear of the unknown in Mars, and fear of the known in Earth, and all there is that will be left behind. Still, there is possibility, something different, something better and something hopeful for their unborn child.

"You sort of have us by the balls, here, right," the husband says. "We can say this isn't right for us, that we still believe in home, and we can leave. But, you know that's crazy talk, that there's nothing to truly go back to, not for long anyway. It's this or what, nothing?"

He takes his wife's hands in his and she begins to tear up.

"Look, we're not interested in your balls," Ricky says, "well, maybe Norrin is…"

They both laugh.

"We are interested in changing lives though, and showing you what's possible," Ricky continues. "This is the future and yes that can be scary, but you're pioneers and you will be building something great, something that lasts and something for your kids and theirs."

They nod.

"If it helps though," I say, "you can have my balls as well. Not only am I married, but I already have a kid, and so I really don't need them anymore."

We all laugh. And then we sign the papers.

26

It is the end of our day and the end of our trip. We have cajoled, manipulated, twisted the truth and created a morphed version of what may or may not be the future as we know it. We have been forceful, seductive, penetrating and dramatic. We have been selling, closing and spinning tales of hopes and dreams that have opened wallets and driven people to invest in a future they cannot quite yet see.

We have done our jobs and we are tired, drained from selling but dialed-up too, full of energy to burn, heads spinning, thoughts cranking, adrenaline coursing, all of it seeking release.

"Gentlemen," the E.C. asks us, "it's been a long trip. Would you like to go back to your room and get some rest before your flight?"

I look at Ricky. I have a package to deliver and it's now or never. I will follow his lead, but eventually I will head out and take care of my business.

"Are you fucking crazy," Ricky says, "we're going out— Good Luck Sector here we come."

I hope we will get some dinner, maybe go shopping— I would like to find a necklace for Shalla and maybe a toy rocket for Joey—but I know better, Ricky clearly has other plans.

"The high-end restaurants and stores are fine, Norrin," Ricky says, "but that's for people who don't know any better. Follow me."

We are soon wandering the back alleys of Good Luck Sector, where the street vendors rule, their little food carts filled with exotic meats from other planets. Fish tacos from Saturn, all flaky and thick; skewers of lamb, or some distant relative of lamb, from Neptune, gamey, but sweet, the grease dripping across our chins; and cold Plutonian yogurt drinks, delicious mixes of fruits previously unknown to me, and highly viscous, which I gulp until my head aches and I start to feel drunk.

As I pause to rub my forehead I see shadows dart across the walls and paths before me and behind me and I begin to wonder if we are being followed, a feeling of paranoia only exacerbated by the vibrations suddenly emanating from Morg's package which is nestled deep in my front pocket.

We walk next toward the Good Luck Sector bazaar and its endless morass of stalls, the space between and around them veering one way and then the next. The bazaar is a chaotic hive of activity, selling, buying, bickering and negotiating.

"This," Ricky says, "is the unacknowledged fuel that drives the machine that is Fu. The workers from across the galaxy who come here, welcomed but not, working clandestinely and at the fringes of what we otherwise sell as an oasis. The cleaners, domestic help, landscapers, servants are all human fodder. They move away from light and exposure by day, and by night they shuffle about down here, selling whatever they can and buying whatever it is they need to get through the week, the month and how ever long they will be needed here."

As Ricky says this, he dramatically sweeps his hands to the left and the right, walking ahead of me, briskly and possessed.

I try to catch up with him, but briefly lose him in the crowd.

I stop to scan the stalls and Morg's box begins to vibrate more intensely, slamming into my thighs. I look to my left and then to my right, and the vibrations begin to crescendo, the box nearly bouncing out of my pocket and onto the ground at my feet.

I walk down one aisle then the next and I soon find myself in the farthest reaches of the bazaar and facing a vendor of undefined place and origin.

"Do you want the kind, this is the kind, the kindest of the kind," the figure under the enormous hood says to me even as I briefly sense movement behind me, and then off to the side.

The vendor is selling variations of SynthKhat that I've never seen in Baidu. The Rings of Saturn, long leaves, purplish green and curling into a circle. Moonbeam, milky white leaves, nearly see-through and luminescent. And Martian Skies, streaky red leaves that go on forever and forever.

"I do want that kind," I say, "but first, I think I have something for you?"

"Of course you do," the vendor says, "give me it please."

I hand him the package and he grabs a handful of SynthKhat from each bin, places it in a bag, hands it to me and bows, before retreating into the back of his stall.

I eat a handful of SynthKhat and move from aisle to aisle looking for Ricky. Soon everything starts to blur together and, as I take one more turn and then another, I find myself on the edges of Happiness Sector.

The bazaar starts to melt away, everything does, the SynthKhat starting to envelope my every thought and movement in a blanket of white noise, my arms heavy, head nodding, legs dragging, but euphoric, at the beginning anyway. The endless series of lights are blinding, eviscerating my ability to fight through the buzz, yet lifting me above Happiness Sector and allowing me to watch the human scrum below as they push their way into the clubs and massage parlors. There are the salesmen looking for that last hit of escape before their long trips home. The soldiers cutting loose, free to roam and shake off the fears that dominate most of their waking moments. The workers seeking release from a life that is all work and little more. The hustlers selling pleasures of all kinds and in all forms. Then, there is me, floating above it all, until this moment, because now I'm coming back to the ground, no longer floating, a sense of dread and paranoia now creeping in. I am so far from home. The faces are so pale. And there is the sense, no, the knowledge that someone, something, is right there, right behind me, no there, beside me, below me, and now I'm bouncing off of people, ping-ponging across the street and seeking some sort of anchor and refuge, before, before what?

"Hey, kid, hey," I hear moments before I realize that Ricky is standing in front of me, "you still with us? What do you say we get a massage? It is our last night here, right?"

"So, you want a massage," a woman says, and where did she come from with her long blue legs, so smooth and cool to the touch?

Do I want a massage and the possibility that I just might be able to relax for a moment and get a taste of what it's like when I catch some wind, the perfect wave, the moment when I can float above and beneath the water all at once?

Maybe?

I follow Ricky into a shop overrun with blue legs and heat.

Ricky immediately gravitates toward the first woman he sees and disappears down a long hall filled with a series of doors covered in Batik sheets.

I grab someone else's hand, not making eye contact, and begin to follow Ricky down the hall, his laughter trailing behind him.

The masseuse and I are about to enter a room when I think about Shalla. Shalla, who I've somehow not thought about all day, or is it days? How, when, did that happen? I don't know, but suddenly I miss her profoundly. It's like a bruise that had slowly been fading until you bump it again, and suddenly the memory of it returns, and it's crushing.

I yank my hand away from the masseuse and I start to run down the hall until I am out of breath and facing a black sheet. I stop for a moment and begin to wonder if this is some kind of trap, whether I have been set up and that after being followed all night, I will step through the curtain only to have someone come up from behind and hit me over the head.

All of this is possible, and yet as I stand there quietly, I hear music—the words are indecipherable, but there is music. Music I now realize that is shaking the walls and the floor beneath me; music that is causing the sheet to flutter ever so slightly like a butterfly's wings; and music that beckons me to step through and become one with the noise.

I step through the curtain.

I have stepped into a karaoke bar, an empty bar except for a handful of waitresses and the occasional dude falling asleep in his seat.

I walk on to the stage and start scrolling through the endless pages of song choices and keep scrolling until I find what I'm looking for and punch in the code.

I munch on the remaining SynthKhat, cramming it into my mouth, and grab the microphone. I look out across the room, remembering what it was like to be on stage, the power and excitement, the nerves and flux. I stand there waiting for Sheena Is a Punk Rocker to begin and when it does I go with it, though tentatively at first.

As the song progresses though, I start to feel the words coursing through my veins and now I'm moving with them, gyrating and pogoing, stomping around and getting loose, a buzz emanating from the song and my skin, everything merging into a sweaty mess.

Soon, I am jumping about and thrashing and leaping as high as I can into the air, before somehow I lose my sense of direction on the way down. I land awkwardly, falling off of the stage and stumbling forward, hoping, wanting to regain my balance, and then I roll into a trot and then a jog as I continue heading right out the front door.

As I slow down I walk right up to the boundary between Happiness Sector and Longevity Sector, where a soldier is standing and waving his rifle, encouraging me to stop walking and turn around, go back where I came from.

I pause, still buzzed, though having shifted from revved-up to lethargy.

As I walk forward, not that I want to, do I, the soldier starts walking toward me as well, mechanical and seething.

For a moment I'm lost in my hazy reflection, but then I see the shadow again, before me, beside me, behind me, everywhere at once, and then the shadow finally emerges, firmly grabs me by the shoulders and spins me around.

"It is time go home brother," George says and I don't argue, instead I just follow him and Dave back to my room.

27

"Just lie back, relax, we are preparing to leave," the calming voice says, still not metallic, or robotic, not scratchy, or booming, just soothing, like rain water, and there for me as I prepare to go home, sleeping, dreaming and spinning across the universe.

I lean my head back, tired and crusty, brain pounding.

"You will soon be asleep," the voice continues, making love to me, always love and goodness, wrapping me in warmth and joy and all the things we want regardless of age.

The voice reminds me first of my mother, it is always the mother, and her creamy softness and flour-specked hair, and then of Shalla who I ache to hold throughout the long night.

"Close your eyes, think good things, happy things," the voice says.

I think of Joey, of walking him to school, laughing together, and watching him grow into a man, someone we can be proud of, someone of worth and deserving of respect.

"You're doing great, just take a deep breath," the voice says as the engines on the shuttle come to life with an enormous hiccup of electricity and fire and life, the slight scent of ethanol wafting past me as I settle back even further into my bed.

I take a deep breath and then another, my eye lids growing heavy and sinking together. I picture myself out at Kanas Lake and on my board as the sun, all orange and streaky red, rises over the gray waters and gray skies, the endless nothingness stretching farther than I can possibly see.

There is movement below me and around me, a slight hum, some grinding, and there is life, the sense of being pushed from below and above all at once, compressed between invisible hands, flattened and stretched, breathe, think good things, kite-surfing, making love, chewing SythKhat on the beach, holding Joey.

28

I am on BeiShan, and there is Al B and I smile, because Al B is there for me, always, the past is the past, this is now, this is new and fresh, and I am in need of something, and he will know what it is. There is history and brotherhood, and love and goodness. Al B waves, greeting me, even as he is talking into a cell phone, waving and talking, and then looking up to the sky above you and beckoning something, what?

I look up. I have to. Al B is not actually waving to me. I hear them before I see them though, and I feel them before they're right there. It's the black helicopters, they have returned; they have found me, and they are coming, their blades spinning, always spinning.

I look at Al B questioning, searching and confused. But he turns away and puts his hand up, his palm facing me and telling me to stop: this is not a betrayal, it is what is has to be. So please, stop looking at him, stop judging him, just stop it all.

I could, I would, I will, I can't, I won't, I'm gone.

I am running home, down the street, everything is cold and gray, the world as we know it is spinning away from us like a top at the edge of a table, hovering, turning, faster, faster, faster, now blurring into nothing, curves and edges, whipping around. This is life, now, then, now. Still running, can't wait to be home, can't wait to hug my mom; as she pulls me to her chest, the smell of vanilla wafts in the air, the flour specking her hair takes flight, bouncing, floating in the shards of sun piercing the kitchen window.

I'm so close, and it's so dark suddenly, and noisy, the

wind whipping my hair this way and that. I look up expecting storm clouds, but no, no, those aren't clouds, they're black helicopters, hovering, watching, and dropping toward me.

Why are they coming down like this? Now I'm running faster. I will get home before they get me and before my mother kills herself. Before the light goes out behind her eyes and she follows my father into wherever the world is where parents go when they're gone—even if they are never truly gone, departed, maybe, removed, no longer present, but still part of your DNA and your life force. No one can take that, and no one can run from it. But I keep running anyway, the blades of the black helicopters nipping at my heels, always just one step behind, and spinning just like I am.

I am no longer so small. Nor am I on the streets of my childhood. Somewhere, somehow, I am running home, home to Shalla. How, why, what? Is Shalla going to kill herself too? I don't know. I don't know who I am, or what I am, or how any of this came to be. I am looking up at my apartment window, and there she is with me, no not me, a version of me, my Terrax me, and they are embracing, they are intertwined, they are kissing.

Briefly they part and Shalla looks at me, no, through me, from the window, a lone tear trickling across her beautiful face. For a moment I believe she will see me, but then she turns away, taking the Terrax's hand and heading toward the back of the apartment and the bedroom.

I need to go to her, run inside, grab her, pin her against the wall and kiss her until her memory has been erased of anything that has happened prior to that very moment. But then, then I look back and the black helicopters haven't budged, and now they're inching forward, and I am running again, away from Shalla, away from home, just away.

I wake-up startled, jolted by fear and confusion and the aching desire to find Shalla, hug her, not let go, and not think about what has been or might still come, just be in the moment, lost in her touch and feel and being home.

What the fuck?

Where am I?

So real.

I awake in a cold sweat.

So real.

I bolt from bed and walk down to the cafeteria where I find Ricky sitting naked except for a towel wrapped around his waist, his saggy man boobs laying there in direct contrast to the taut skin stretched across his suddenly ancient face. He is like a statue, aged and wise from afar, but less vibrant and crumbling up close.

"Hey kid, you look like you've seen a ghost," Ricky says sipping his coffee briefly before adding, "and I don't mean me."

"It's the dreams," I say sitting down across from him, "they're so vivid, so real, but not remotely a reflection of anything I've ever seen. They're more like something I might see, or could see. That's fucked up, right?"

Ricky smiles.

"Hey E.C.," Ricky shouts, "how about some Synth-Khat?"

"Yes sir," the E.C. says, the metallic burp echoing across the otherwise quiet room.

An arm extends from the table and two small bowls of SynthKhat are deposited in front of us. We both take a handful and start to eat, Ricky popping chunks in his mouth like he's eating peanuts at a bar.

"It's called 'dream forward' Norrin," Ricky says. "On

the return trip your dreams accelerate. They are the vapor trails of experiences still to be lived, lingering and swirling into a crazy quilt vision of some version of your life that's yet to happen."

"I don't want what I've seen," I say my legs and arms starting to feel numb.

"You never do," Ricky says looking wired, "but you have to block it out, accept it, there's no controlling it. Look at Shelley that sorry motherfucker. He never could accept it, any of it."

"What does that mean?" I say.

"Nothing, never you mind," Ricky says looking away.

"What if you just say no?" I say my heading throbbing and feeling desperate. "What if you can't take it, don't want to take it and just walk?"

"You can't do that kid," Ricky says, "no walking, you're in. This is it."

"I'm not sure I can do that," I say as I begin repetitively drumming my fingers on the table and thinking, this is your brain on drugs, this, now. "The dreams, being away from Shalla and Joey, the relentless need to focus on work, the fear and confusion, and the jealousy, this is not the kind of life I wanted."

"Get some sleep Norrin," Ricky says, "you'll feel better, and then we'll be home and that stuff will drift away. You'll make it drift away, memories lost to time, and some place you once were but aren't any more."

"You promise?" I say now winding down as quickly as I was winding up.

"Yeah kid, I promise," Ricky says sighing, "now go back to bed—re-entry can be an ass-fuck and better to sleep through it."

And so I do.

29

Thunk.

Huh?

There is grinding, metal on metal, and mashing, on my head and in the air, everywhere. It is familiar, mostly, confusing still, but I've been here, there, here. There is settling, lowering, movement, shaking and more grinding, scratching and pings. While I don't know exactly what's happening, some part of me does know, and something will turn on soon, has to, will.

The movement is slowly coming to a halt. I am here, somewhere, yes, here, somewhere. But where, is it Kanas Lake? What, I don't know? I know I cannot breathe, but I will, I know I will, and I will calm down. I will, right, right.

I try get up, but, what, oh, the lights are coming on. The glare burns my eyes, my skin, my brain. I put my hand up in front of my face, shielding myself from that which I don't yet grasp, but will soon, now, yes.

"Relax, breathe," the calming voice says, always calm, always protective, like a cocoon.

I relax.

I breathe.

"Slowly move your hands and feet," the voice continues, "you are alright."

How does she know this? Because she is the voice and I know to trust the voice. The voice loves me, and the voice knows everything. I trust that and know it to be unequivocally true. It has to be so.

I shake my hands and feet, at first just moving millimeters at a time, and then something more, bending, and blood flow. My eyes begin to adjust, my brain no longer so fried, my skin beginning to cool.

"You are here," the voice says, and the voice is life, "the journey is complete, please stand-up, slowly."

I am home.

Soon, I will see Joey and Shalla, and I will wallow in them and lose myself in them and ultimately engulf them so there is nothing left that I will ever need.

I tell my legs to stand, to swing over the side of the bed, but they do not, will not, not at first. I know it's possible though and I push off of the bed, despite peeing my pants, and despite the jolt that ripples through my legs, starting with my feet, before moving through my calves, knees, thighs and into my hips.

I know I can do it, and now I'm standing. I'm good. As good as I can be.

"Please proceed to the shower station outside the shuttle door," the voice says.

30

I emerge from the shower, balanced and clear, all synapses firing, muscles and organs in synch, energy coursing, and excitement about getting back and heading home. I will enjoy this time off, time well-earned, a successful trip behind me, and more to come, soon, maybe. But not so soon, this is my time.

I pause to look out of the window in the terminal the vast expanse of Baidu looming off in the distance, my home nestled in there and waiting for my return. I'm almost there, so close and free to be with my family; a brief respite from obligation, work, the Corporation, my debts, all of it. It's time to reconnect, banishing the memories and dreams of this trip and all that comes with them, the isolation, the confusion and fear.

"Hello, Norrin," a familiar voice says from behind me, "welcome home."

I turn around and find myself face to face with Morg. Fuck, motherfucker, fuck, so close, so fucking close. Goddamn you Morg you baby-faced motherfucker.

"Nice to see you Morg," I say forcing a smile, and ready to act out, relinquishing all control over my feelings and unwilling to care that I'm doing so, "I didn't know they had you working the greeting committee as well. Nice."

"It's Steven," he says with his pink baby-faced half-grimaced, half-suppressed smile. "Now please come follow me, let's talk."

We walk into a room similar to the one we first met in. Sparse. Windowless. A table and a few chairs. There is no box in the middle of the table though, no clip for my finger, no nothing.

"What, no clip Steven?" I say sitting down and looking at Morg. "You have nothing to probe? No truths to seek out, nothing about my disappeared father or dead mother? What about the lingering effects of those losses and their impact on my psyche? Or, wait for it, my feelings toward the Corporation regarding my ability to move huge parcels of property?"

Morg smiles, he adjusts his baby-faced head, first left, then right; he purses his lips and squints. He starts to speak. He stops. He's thinking. I can see him thinking, the circuits firing, the engines whirring. What's right he's wondering, what's the best approach to this conversation, the right mix of fear and humor?

He smiles. And then he starts again.

"Why would we need the clip?" Morg says. "Do you have something to hide?"

This is fun. Morg has no real advantage this time—he knows everything; I know he knows everything and so now I can just fuck with him.

"You tell me?" I respond.

What could he say? There are no secrets. I sold property. I moved his package. I munched SynthKhat. I sang karaoke. I came back. And now I'm going home. End of discussion.

"Are you enjoying yourself?" Morg says suddenly getting serious.

I look at him quizzically, but don't speak, he seems upset. I want the moment to last just a little longer.

"Is this a joke to you?" Morg shouts, suddenly reaching out, grabbing my wrists and pulling me toward him.

I wrench my arms free and smile at him. Fucker. Morg leans back in his chair, takes a deep breath, a sole bead of sweat forming along his forehead.

"We're building something great here," he continues, more calmly now, chilly, composed. "We've invited you to be part of something so much bigger than you, so much bigger than you deserve, and you will respect it."

I lean forward, looking for something in Morg's face, a tell of some kind, and some kind of insight into the hand he's playing. There's always an angle, something hidden, an agenda. It's never just passion, is it?

We look at one other, sizing each other up. What's the move?

"I will respect it or what?" I respond. "Are you going to make me disappear too, like father, like son?"

"Hey, I was just kidding," Morg says relaxing his shoulders, "I kid, I thought you would enjoy me playing bad cop."

I don't speak. I don't believe him. And I don't speak. Let him think he's in charge.

"And this disappeared nonsense, the Corporation doesn't do that," Morg says, "never did, and you will never hear otherwise. But now that you've had your fun, please report to the office."

What, now? Why? I want to go home, fuck, fuck, fuck, it's time to go home, and I can't be apart from Shalla for one more moment. Who knows what's going on there, went on there and may still go on there. Fuck, Morg must know how much I care about this. Of course, he does, he knows what matters to me. My sense of loss, my fear of betrayal, and the ongoing belief that things just blow-up, just like that, have to, that's how it works.

Motherfucker.

I'm not ready to let go though, not ready to relinquish my moment of control, much less try to reign in my growing sense of dread.

"And if I just go home?" I ask.

"It's a simple request," Morg says now leaning forward himself, "a brief stop and nothing worth making a stand over. Though feel free to, what could happen, right?"

Right.

"Fine Steven, I'll go," I say. "It's cool. We're cool. One more thing, what about my debt to you, are we square?"

"Not by a long shot bitch," Morg replies, "see ya."

31

I step into my pod as I prepare to take the train to BeiShan. The pod is filled with ghosts, ethereal and momentary, all passing through this world and this time for the briefest of stops. The universe started here, or there, and continues on from there, or here, to there or here, always moving, always suffering rebuilding, rethinking its mistakes, and compensating for its endless flaws, everything moving forward though. Sometimes by leaps and bounds, other times more tediously, and death and life and birth and growth—all of it blurs as we progress. And so really who are these ghosts to my left and right? They may leave something behind, but more likely they will be forgotten, what remains little more than memory and dust.

The train rolls into BeiShan and my pod locks into the station awaiting my release. As I depart I look out over the neighborhood, the hustlers and thieves, the vendors and the nuts, the poets and SynthKhat dealers, the grid-faced police and endlessly hovering black helicopters.

They are all ghosts too, here now, and then gone, because that's where it all goes, nowhere, and everywhere. Today the Earth, tomorrow Mars, after that Venus, or somewhere still undiscovered. Everything gets destroyed, consumed and subsumed, and then we move on, and on, and on; and so here, now, I must be in it, before I become a ghost as well.

I walk up to the office door, still nondescript and still hidden in plain sight. A helicopter swoops by overhead, as always, briefly pausing, but then moving on just as quickly as it appeared. I place my hand squarely against the scanner next to the door and feel the laser glide over and around the curlicues in my fingertips and the endlessly arching cracks and folds of my palms. When the green light blinks I lean forward and allow the eye scanner to pass before and across my eyes, first right to left, followed by a puff of air, then left to right, pause, another puff of air before the scanner's beams stop to linger, boring their way into the deep recesses of my eyes, until all involved are satisfied that I am Norrin Radd, no more, no less.

The door snaps open, I walk in and approach the front desk where the E.C. with the sweet ass awaits me.

"Hey handsome," the E.C. says, "I've been patiently waiting for you to return, but it hasn't been easy. It gets lonely here when you're not around."

"Yeah," I say, "you stayed faithful though, right, tell me you did. I did."

"You know I did," the E.C. says almost purring.

A scantily dressed Terrax walks by and I turn to look.

"Hey," the E.C. says, "eyes forward, that's not cool."

"You're right," I say, "but you're so hot I need a distraction or I may just forget I'm a married man."

"Good save Sailor," the E.C. says, "they're waiting inside for you."

"Until next time," I say.

"Can't wait," the E.C. says as I walk past her and into the coffee room.

Sitting around the table are Ricky, Shelley and John, all waiting for me, and knowing everything, and nothing, all at once.

"There he is," Ricky shouts clapping his hands.

"How you doing kid? good to see those ancient shuttles can still get the job done," Shelley says, his old-man smell still permeating the space between us.

"This guy is all about the close," Ricky says jumping up, "you should have seen him—he's a rock star, a fucking rock star."

"You've got the gift," Shelley says, "and it is a gift, it doesn't matter how you got here, only what you do when you're through the door."

"And you are through the door," Ricky says. "Mazel tov, genius."

John isn't saying anything, just watching, slightly bemused, slightly annoyed, bound to kill this conversation at any moment.

"You get to go home too, don't you kid," Shelley says, "that's nice."

"Right," Ricky says, "your kid, your own bed, your woman, beautiful, well-earned and beautiful."

"And nothing to worry about," Shelley says, his voice slightly cracking, "it's all good—your woman, home, nothing to worry about there, never."

"It may be odd at first kid, time passes, there are changes, sometimes subtle, mostly negligible, nothing really…," Ricky says almost wistfully before trailing off.

"The main thing," Shelley says, his voice rising, "is not to focus on your Terrax—he's gone, and he's nothing."

Shelley starts to rub his forehead, he closes his eyes, and looks anguished, pained, and suddenly very old, ancient, just a shell of something that maybe once was filled with vigor but isn't any more.

Ricky reaches over and touches his shoulder, giving him a squeeze.

"Enough," John says smiling, "it's time to celebrate."

With that, John snaps his fingers and three female Terraxes walk in and start dancing in front of us, their clothes rapidly coming off, their nearly real skin slightly aglow.

John passes around a bowl of SynthKhat as the Ter-raxes continue to dance before us. As we slowly consume the entire bowl, the girls blur, morph and bend, my legs start to hum then melt, and I see Shelley bury his face in his hands and start to cry, first softly, then more intensely. Ricky pats him on the back, whispers something in his ear and watches wistfully as Shelley, shoulders slumped walks off toward the back of the office.

For a moment, Ricky looks sad, and old, not fake or smiling, just beaten down. But only for a moment—soon he is electric again, grabbing the hand of a blonde Ter-rax and heading over to the men's room, all smiles and unnecessary charm, talking a mile a minute, now more cartoon than man, all wistfulness kicked to the curb.

Watching Ricky I briefly forget how fucked up I am, but then a red-haired Terrax plants herself on my lap and I remember that I am still in the coffee room, as is John who has a black-haired Terrax sitting on his lap, grinding and rotating, all fake moans and fake breaths. He seems happy, though as bristly as ever.

I should focus on my lap dance, but I instead find that I can't stop focusing on John.

When my mother killed herself, John offered me a handshake, firm, terse, no reaction. Not a word, and for second, I almost cried, his stiffness and inability to ac-knowledge something as real as death and loss, somehow more difficult to roll with than any of the people crying and wanting to hug me. Their reactions weren't real to me. They were performances, mother dead, parentless child, be sad, demonstrate something, anything. Let him know you care. Show him that you feel his pain and that you are here for him—in this moment, be here, right here and sad.

But not John, there was no performance, no emotion, cut off possibly from his feelings, and anyone else's, certainly, but not pretending either. No games, no effort to be something he was not nor will ever be.

Guys like that are great for running things and they're certainly perfect to work for the Corporation. No work for the unwashed and unwanted, that's fine for them, because they have no feelings about how any of this affects anything anyway.

It's about progress, development, looking forward and taking care of your friends and those who ensure your stay in power. Which John gets and which besides his father's connections, is why John is here. He can run things without emotion, but more importantly he knows what's expected and who needs to be taken care of. And it isn't us.

I don't realize that I'm staring at John until he says, "What do you want Norrin? You're killing my buzz and my hard-on. Fuck."

"What's up with Shelley?" I say, not even knowing I've been thinking about him until find myself asking the question.

John looks at me, through me, sizing me up. To him I will never truly be anything but the fatherless loser he knew, ignored and sometimes bullied in high school. But that doesn't mean I can't do the job, and since the job must be done I deserve some modicum of respect for that reason alone.

"Here's the thing Norrin," John says, "Shelley never recovered from his last trip, the endless dreams of Terraxes fucking his precious fucking wife, and the visions of her killing herself because of that. He can't shake that fucking image, and so while it's true that the Corporation knows what to do to protect the spouses of space salesmen, we really don't know who can handle space travel until they go, though even then, no one can handle it for long."

I notice at this point, that John is doing his best to say everything calmly and matter of factly, which is impressive when you consider that a naked Terrax is still writhing away on his lap.

"So, what does all of this mean?" John continues. "It means that Shelley is a whack job, off his rocker, and broken. It means that he doesn't sell any more, because he can't be fixed. He just comes to work, or more accurately, he just stays here, while his wife lives with his Terrax and then that Terrax's Terrax and on and on. Ironic right? At some point, Shelley will truly spin out of control, no longer even able to pretend to himself that he's at work, that he's stable, and that he's worth something. And when that happens, we will send him off to the territories to fend for himself, or maybe to Kanas Lake where they will take him in as long as he can last there."

John lifts the Terrax off of his lap and she walks away and toward his office.

"It also means that all of you are disposable," John says waving his hand around the room, "which is just how the Corporation likes it."

John stands up.

"I guess it means something else as well," John says finally smiling, "while you're really fucking valuable to me right now, at some point you won't be. But for now you are, and you're mine, questions?"

Questions, I don't know? Choose one, any one. Am I to understand that I too will find myself spinning out of control at some point? That Shalla will eventually find herself living with my Terrax, raising our child with my

Terrax and fucking my Terrax? That no one cares about any of this? That the Corporation deems us expendable and that there is nothing I can do about it, so really why ask anything at all?

John looks at me. He's stone faced, but I know he must be enjoying this on some level. Yes, he has numbers to hit, and there are expectations and a job to do, but this here, this moment, also serves to remind him, and me, that we all have our role in society and that these roles don't change much. When you are born to be in charge, you are always in charge, and someone like me can try to be cool, or rebellious—hustle, chew SynthKhat, and sleep with anyone who will let me, even if or when that someone is the girlfriend of my best, only, friend—but ultimately I will gain little in terms of power, cache or influence. Any freedom, liberation or creativity I achieve is only going to be in my head, because if there is any real freedom to be given out, it is given to the Johns, and Morgs, of the world from birth, and all they need to do is tend to it.

"No questions," John says, "why doesn't that surprise me? You never cared much about anything, did you?"

What's the right response to that I wonder, and what response would John even care about if I had one to offer him?

"I care about my family," I say quietly, though still trying to sound forceful.

"That's nice," John says, "and you're taking care of them now. You're good at selling, man, I will give you that. I don't get it, but I don't have to."

"That almost sounded like a compliment," I say, "backhanded maybe, but still, I will take what I can get."

"That seems consistent," John says, "and look, I do want you to go and enjoy your family because we need you to go back. People want this property, the market is primed, and it is all hands on deck."

I don't know what this means, but the SynthKhat is definitely wearing off, and the anxiety is starting to wrap itself around my brain.

"Okay," I say, "but how does that work? We never really talked about it. How do you decide when someone goes back? because right now I can't imagine doing so."

"I understand," John says. "And look, take today, tonight, tomorrow morning even, but we need you back at Arthur Chin tomorrow night."

Tomorrow night? I recoil. Did I hear that right? I grip the arm rests on my chair. How am I going to explain that to Shalla and Joey? I close my eyes and loosen my neck. This isn't what I signed on for, is it? I don't want this.

Hold on. Concentrate on something good—surfing, Joey, Shalla's hair, thighs and neck.

"Tomorrow," I finally say, "really, how?"

"What did you think?" John says. "This is the job. People would kill you for it, people outside this very door. And if you don't care about that, I know you care about your family, your obligations to them, and your debt to Steven. Yes, I know about that, and so my question is, are you ready to turn your back on all of this? Can you?"

I don't respond.

"I didn't think so," John says, "tomorrow night sport-o. Now go enjoy your time off."

32

I drift off of the train, in and out of Bao and then into the neighborhood where the usual group of jobless, yet suited, ghosts wander by wide-eyed and dazed; random Terraxes run out of steam and stop dead in their tracks, only to be picked up for parts by the everpresent E.C.s; and a flash mob of black-clothed kids appear as if from the ether, holding their places as long as they can before the black helicopters swoop-in.

It is a reminder that things never quite change, not noticeably, subtly maybe, incrementally certainly, but mostly they hold steady; it's the way of the world.

I wonder what that means for Ricky, Shelley and me, and what that means about work, because I can't imagine going back so soon, and I can't imagine how that will change by tomorrow.

And then I'm home, really home. I stop out front. I take a deep breath. I walk in.

"Hello, sir," E.C. says, "welcome home."

It seems odd to think of E.C. as a friendly face, but he does represent home, and seeing him means I've made it back, for now.

"Hello E.C.," I respond, "how have you been? You look like you lost some weight."

"Very funny sir," E.C. says, "Shalla is out getting Joey as we speak. Are you thinking of making something special?"

"Yes, I am, lobster, actually, they had some nice-looking ones at Bao," I say raising the bag in my hand to eye level. "I'm also thinking about macaroni and cheese for Joey."

"Good choices sir," E.C. replies, "and don't forget, Shalla likes just a splash of butter sauce with her lobster and Joey likes his macaroni and cheese baked."

"Ha-ha, I think I know that, anything else I should know?" I say, forcing myself to laugh, because I do know that, don't I? I don't know.

"No sir, I started boiling some water for you, but otherwise, I think you got it; now relax, you will be fine, they will be fine," E.C. says.

"Thanks E.C.," I say as I turn toward the elevator and head up to the apartment.

Once inside I head to the kitchen and go about making dinner. I place the lobsters in the large pot of boiling water in front of me and then the macaroni in the sauce pan next to that.

"Small sauce pan please," I say, "and some butter."

The metallic arm extends from the slot and places the sauce pan on a free burner. The arm retreats back into slot and re-emerges with some butter it places into the sauce pan.

"Let's also do some asparagus please," I say.

"Yes sir, and how about some Hollandaise sauce to go with that," E.C. asks, "Shalla likes that as well."

Of course she does. I knew that too, right?

"Of course," I say, which is how I continue as we prepare dinner, dutiful, efficient, focused, never thinking about what has occurred while I was gone, much less what is to come when Shalla and I actually see each other, or the fact that I will be leaving again tomorrow.

I also try to ignore the fact that I don't quite trust that I still know my own family. That somehow during the time that passed when I was away I either forgot the pertinent facts about our lives, their likes and dislikes, their fears and joys, or that maybe those facts have changed.

I may be ready to pick right up where we left off, but that doesn't mean they are as well. On some level, I fear they are not who I think they are, or worse, that what I think I know is a construct of my own making, and mine alone.

"Daaaaaaaaaaaaaaaaaaaaaaaaaady!"

Joey is tearing into the kitchen, hugging me, climbing up my legs and springing into my now-waiting arms. I squeeze him until he tries to wrestle free, nuzzling his awesome five-year-old neck, smelling his five-year-old skin and running my fingers through his hair. Does he seem taller? Thinner? Has he lost more of his baby fat? And baby teeth, are there any missing, has anything come in? I keep searching, wondering, trying to figure out what if anything has changed, but it's not clear, and this is good I think. We're cool, right? Yes.

"What did you bring me?" Joey asks, having wriggled free and landed in front of me, hands on his hips, shoulders squared, a half smile covering his little pumpkin head.

I fish out the rocket ship I bought him at the bazaar.

"How's this?" I say.

"Awesome," he says, grabbing it before proceeding to run around the house and jump onto the furniture, rocket in hand as it soars through galaxies only Joey fully knows.

"Please be careful Joey," I hear E.C. say in the background as Shalla turns the corner and walks into the kitchen.

I lose my breath for a moment, just as I always do after any kind of break.

She is glowing, her long, honey hair cascading onto a long, flowing multicolored dress that just covers her wonderful hips and bosom, their silhouettes just noticeable beneath the gauzy, near see-through material I picture tearing off right here, right now. She's like a goddess. She is a goddess. My goddess and I don't have to share her with anyone.

"What did you get me?" she says breaking into a big smile as she walks toward me.

I reach out hands first and cup her face and we start to kiss. Everything goes black, except for the stars exploding in my brain, and soon we are spinning around the kitchen, and then out the window and across the universe, two people lost in one another and dancing to their own song. This goes on for seconds, minutes, forever—I don't know, don't care. Everything and everyone everywhere else is gone now, disappeared, and we are all that exists.

"Sir," a voice says from somewhere across space and time immemorial.

I ignore the voice, but I am already losing my grip on the moment. We are no longer in space, the real world trickling back in like a slow bleed just before a stroke.

"Sir," E.C. says, "I'm sorry to disturb you, but the Hollandaise sauce is about to burn."

I pull away from Shalla and turn my attention back to the stove. I lift the sauce pan with the now bubbling Hollandaise sauce off of the burner and place it on the counter.

"You couldn't deal with that yourself E.C.?" I say. "We were kind of having a moment."

"I didn't want to be pushy sir," E.C. replies.

33

Dinner is eaten. The table is cleared. Dishes washed. And I am lying in bed with Joey reading Where The Wild Things are.

"How come there isn't a dad?" Joey asks.

"I don't know," I say, "I never noticed that."

"Do you think he is traveling for a work vacation?" Joey says.

"He might be," I say, "dads do what they have to for their families. That's part of what makes them dads."

"Like you," he says.

"Yes, exactly," I say, rolling over and laying my head on his shoulder.

"And it's not because you don't love us," Joey says, "or would rather be somewhere else, right?"

"No, never," I say, "you and your mom are the best things that ever happened to me."

"But you could do something closer to home, couldn't you?" Joey says.

"I'm not sure baby, should I look into that?" I say, trying to fight the feeling of impossibility that immediately creeps into my brain.

"Yes, okay, whatever," he says getting drowsy.

It is now, right now, that I'm supposed to tell him that I'm leaving again, but I don't, can't, I'm too chicken.

"Tell me about your dad," he says, his eyes closing and dreamy.

"I didn't really know him," I say.

"I would hate that," Joey says curling away from me and facing the wall.

"Me too," I say as he falls asleep, "me too…"

34

As the moonlight slices through the window and across our bed, Shalla and her nakedness are wrapped in the sheets next to me, some parts illuminated, others shrouded in shadow. There is a sliver of shoulder, the outside curve of her breast, the bottom of her knee, a touch of ankle and a glimpse of her forearm.

The rest of her is lost, buried, present, not exposed to the elements, only to some of my senses. Shalla is like a ghost, a beautiful, semipresent apparition, who with each move, each role and twist, is a little more and a little less all at once.

What I can see though is Shalla absentmindedly fingering the necklace I brought her home. I run my finger across her shoulder and it pops with static electricity.

"You didn't have to do this," she says rolling toward me, "but I'm glad you did."

I stroke her cheek, my obsession with her glowing skin as strong as ever. I start to kiss her neck, tasting her still-drying sweat and smelling the sex still lingering on her. I slip my hand down to her still-wet thighs and roll on top of her, her legs parting, welcoming me in.

I should have my eyes closed, but instead I try to keep them open, wanting to take in the moment and her, all of her—the slight scar just below the tip of her chin, the faded birthmark on her right hip. And as she starts to move with me, then lift, I keep my eyes open because I will be gone again tomorrow and I do not want to lose a single second, or forget a thing. I need this, or need to need it, but recognizing this means I have to think about what tomorrow will bring. About leaving again and how I don't want to tell her about it.

Soon the dread starts to build in my chest and then my shoulders. I try to loosen my neck, but this just makes me lose my momentum and alter our rhythm. I hope we can recover and I'm still going, moving and thrusting, sliding, but whatever we might have had is gone, my actions now force of habit, muscle memory, and not remotely arousing.

I can't tell if she can tell that I'm distracted, but I am— all the things I could ignore before are now conspiring against my focus and timing. The sheets are tangled and chafing. The sweat on my brow is lingering there, heavy and burning. My back is sore. And I am lost, not concentrating and not into it any more.

I need to talk to her, tell her what's about to happen. It's so hard though, telling her something that will upset her, that will leave her feeling abandoned like my mom felt. Because when things get like that, things implode, they have to, and there's no way around it.

I don't want this, but I don't know what to do to prevent it, and I never have.

"What?" Shalla says.

I look down. I have closed my eyes after all, lost in trying to concentrate. Her skin is now make-up free, her freckles just floating there and as always collecting under her nose in an awesome cluster of brown on brown on brown.

"I think I lost you there for a moment buddy," she says now sliding out from under me, her slick skin, frictionless and smooth. "Are you alright?"

I should know what to say, loving someone means knowing what to say, or at least knowing how to fix something after you've broken it. I don't know how to do either though, and because of this I am not a good partner to her. I am a good provider and I would not go anywhere away from her and Joey out of choice. I know this, and I don't have a choice if I'm going to do what's needed. Do I? I don't know. And I don't know what I know, except that I should be able to communicate this, and that I love her, them, but I don't know how to do this, any of it.

Instead I am about to break something and I know it, but feel powerless to prevent it. I am going to say the wrong thing and even though I can see the words forming on the tip of my tongue and even though I have a chance to reel them back in, capture them, make them go away and prevent myself from doing something the wrong way, I will say these words anyway. And I will do so, because it's easier to do the wrong thing, and if I admit it to myself, it's also easier to leave when you've fucked things up.

But I can't admit that to myself, much less the fact that what I am about to say, and keep saying, is all about my fears, insecurities and confusion, the tangled layers of my bullshit, and not hers, not hers at all.

"What?" Shalla says more firmly, looking at me, "now you're just acting weird?"

"Tell me about him," I say, "I really want to know."

"Who?" Shalla says accusingly, "what, is this about Al B? Aren't we done talking about him?"

It always comes back to him. To her it does. I stole her and I hurt him. Though let's be honest, she fucked him, and who cares if it was before I met her, or that I was there at other times when he did, I can't handle it, I need her to be mine.

Of course that's the thing, it's not about Al B, it's about these kinds of feelings maybe, but not him, and she must know this, right? Yes, but if she does, what does that mean? Is she holding out on me? Is she trying to make me say something I don't want to say? Testing me, forcing me to spar like this? What? Or does she really not know?

Then again, whatever she thinks, or doesn't think, why am I letting this happen regardless?

"No," I say, "I'm over that. Al B's the past, he's nothing. You know what I'm asking."

"Do I?" she says looking at me incredulously.

Is she for real? And can I please stop this now, please?

"I know what you want me to talk about," she says, "and I know it's not about Al B, not entirely. I get it. What I don't understand is why you care more about that than me and what it's like not having you here? The confusion and the fear and the caring for Joey all by myself when you know that I never even wanted him, or this. That I wasn't ready, but that I love him now so much, and that he was so important to you that I would do anything for him, just like I would do anything for you."

"Hey…," I start to say, wanting to console her, say the right thing, something.

"No," Shalla says, "let me finish, you never ask me how I feel about anything. It's all some fucking fantasy for you. The family you did not have. No mess, no fear, no loss. You want to provide for us, I know that, I do, but what about my feelings? What about what I want and need and who I might be? I went from being my dad's possession to Al B's to yours—trapped, preserved, a trophy. It doesn't work like that, it can't. We need to talk, and you need to try and understand me."

"I can, I will," I say and I mean it, really, "go ahead, I'm listening."

"Having the Terrax here, it's like living with a ghost, no like living in a dream, perpetually sleeping," Shalla says, "bouncing from one variation of the same dream to the next. You know things are not quite real, not wrong or bad, just not real. And yet everything is almost identical, the mannerisms, the affect in the Terrax's voice, the ways he seems to know me, my past, where I get tripped-up, or scared, what makes me happy or brings me pleasure. With Joey of course, it's like a Godsend, because with Joey, he's all patience and calm. Of course that's when he's most fake, or off, because no parent is like that, it's impossible, not real. But that's the thing, none of it is real, and ultimately there's a wall that can't be penetrated. Nothing is raw or exposed—human—and that's what I love about you, about us, it's real. Sometimes too real, the anger and confusion, your inability to say what's haunting you, but there's passion as well, and that cannot be replaced. You cannot be replaced."

For a moment, I am lost in Shalla's words, her emotion, and for a moment, I'm so close, so close to ignoring all my fears and craziness, centered and exposed, and ready, and I love her so much. But then, just when it seems that we're about to right the ship and avoid the edge of the cliff, things start to spin out of control, and I spin away from all that's possible.

"I don't want to replace you," Shalla continues, "you won me, I'm yours for keeps, and you're home, here, right here, and we have the chance to do something different, be something different. Can we be something different?"

Why, why did she have to mention that I'm home, like it's permanent, like we have time to figure things out, because it's not, and we don't. I want this not to bother me, that all of this is so temporary and fleeting—not just us, here, my time home, but everything. Because it's all endlessly snatched from our hands, and now just like that, we're right back where we, I, was, dreading what I need to say and knowing I'm about to break something, us, all of it.

"What?" she says, so beautiful and so right.

We could be different, we could, and yet all I know is death and destruction and if that's all you know how can you hope things will go differently?

Still, I know enough to know that we could stop it here. We could be okay. We could be something good, if even for a moment, and it's all right here and right in my hands. This is my moment for greatness, but apparently I'm not made for greatness, not by a long shot.

"I'm glad we're talking," I say, "I am, but you have to tell me more about him, I want to know more, something, anything."

Shalla recoils and then rights herself.

"Your Terrax?" she says shaking her head. "After all of that, he's all you want to talk about? Why, what else is there to say?"

"You tell me," I reply.

"What," she says, "it was nothing. It was like having you here, but not exactly, I already said that."

"Not exactly—how could you tell the difference? I understand it's pretty tough," I say, thinking about how he knew how to bring her pleasure, pleasure, why use that word?

"I can tell the difference," Shalla says defensively, "and I'm not sure what it is or how, but it was different, really, I swear."

"Me thinks the lady doth protest too much," I say, "and I don't care, really."

"Really," Shalla says, "you don't care, its sort of hard to tell at the moment."

And now it's a showdown, started by me, my weakness,

my inability to be something, forthright, mature, pick anything.

"No," I say, "I don't care, unless you fucked him. Did you?"

There it is, the door is open, and it will never close again.

"Jesus," Shalla says, "you're joking right?"

"Of course," I say, and as I say this, I know that I'm lying to her, and myself, because at this moment, I am hit with a realization as pure and painful as any I have ever experienced. I want to believe that somehow this is all about jealousy and pettiness, and the idea that I will not share her, cannot share her. But it's not about any of that. I have to leave again and I believe that might destroy her. And because I cannot bear thinking about that, much less telling her the truth and finding out how she will react, I'd rather let her think that I am paranoid and small and unable to be the kind of man she deserves.

"Good, then I should be honest," Shalla says, "I did fuck him, and it was great, better even than being with you. Are you happy to know that?"

What I know is that she's just trying to make her hurt go away, but I also know that whatever might have happened here is dead, done, fucked and destroyed, by me.

And yet, even as I know this, and even as I know I caused it, I hate her for not knowing why I said what I said and acted as I did. I hate her for taking the bait and somehow not being better than me. Mostly though, I hate myself and my inability to express my fears to her, and this self-hatred quickly mutates into rage, and the rage needs an outlet, and she looks up at me, so sad and vulnerable, which makes me hate her more, and I suddenly want to punch her in her beautiful face, break it and break her, right here.

I feel my hands hardening into fists, and my chest starts to tighten. I look for something else to hit, turning here, there, and here again. But there is nowhere to turn. The room is contracting around us, the walls and ceiling caving in, even as the bed is swallowing us whole.

"I don't know what to say," Shalla says grabbing me and crying, "and I don't know what you want me to say, but I'll say this, the whole thing is a blur. When you left, when he arrived, and when you came back. Its seamless and it all flows together, and I don't know what I've done or not done, but you're here now and that's all that counts right?, right?, say something."

But I'm not here, and won't be, and so I focus on steadying myself, and I think about my mom and space and hitting the waves I am going to have to hit soon if I'm going to keep my shit together. I can almost concentrate again, almost, and Shalla starts to hug me, and I breathe, slowly, in and out, and Shalla is kissing me, and talking, repeating again and again, "I don't know what happened, I don't know, it's all a blur, all a blur."

And now we're making love again, and as we find the rhythm that eluded us earlier, a line from a story I read so long ago pops into my heads, "I would prefer not to."

"I would prefer not to."

It sums it all up. I would prefer not to be who I am tonight. I would prefer not to be so scared of hurting Shalla when I should probably trust that she's strong enough not to be broken by my absence. And I would prefer not to be the worker I am expected to be. Shalla and Joey are more important to me than Mars, a good job, my debt, or my fears.

I would also prefer to not to say anything to Shalla about any of this, which is fucked up and backwards and the antithesis of everything else I'm saying to myself. I'm not ready to be the person I might be. I am still the person who destroyed everything tonight and that's not going to change, not yet, and maybe ever, though I hope that's not true.

"Hey," I say, not looking at her, just staring at the ceiling as the sun comes up, "I need to leave again for work, today, I'm sorry, but I'll be back soon, promise."

Then I get up and I don't look back, I'm too ashamed.

35

I am outside the building, the sun still rising, a splash of orange and red, with tendrils of purple creeping across the otherwise gray sky and stretching over the massiveness of Kanas Lake. I have my board on my shoulder and my bags are sitting in the lobby awaiting my return. I know E.C. can't feel anything, but it's hard not to think that he looked sad when I left, and while it may just be the guilt, I know it wasn't because I was leaving, but because of how I treated Shalla and how different it could have been.

Joey is kicking along beside me and I am going to drop him off at school before I hit the waves, the shuttle, and Mars.

"Hey buddy," I say, "as we were sort of talking about last night, I need to go to work again today, but I will be home soon."

"Okay," he says, "will you bring me another rocket?"

"Yeah," I say, "of course. I also have a big favor to ask you, alright?"

"Okay," he says, looking up at me with this big brown eyes, "what?"

"I need you to be the man of the house while I'm gone," I say.

"What do you mean," he says, "you're still here even when you're gone."

"Yeah," I say choking-up, "how so?'

Joey stops walking and takes my hand.

"You know, you're here to walk me to school, or hug me when I'm sad," he says.

"Is that good?" I say.

"Sure," he says, "but you don't smell like you, or hug quite the same way, and mommy cries more. She misses you, you you, you know?"

I start to cry and quickly wipe the tears so Joey won't see me.

"Look buddy," I say, leaning down to his level and lightly gripping his shoulders, "I really love you guys, and I will be home soon okay? I promise to be home soon, so you keep an eye on mommy for me, deal?"

"If you promise to bring me another rocket," he says.

"Done," I say hugging him a little too hard.

"I can't breathe daddy," Joey says.

I let go of him and watch as Joey runs into school, enters his cubicle and puts on his headphones. I then watch him for a moment as he begins his lesson.

"ei, bi, xi…"

36

When nothing else makes sense there are the waves, and in the waves there is Zen—balance and understanding, recognition of problems and the untangling of confusions. There is also the sense that we are just small parts of a much bigger universe. Specks in time and space, insignificant really, except to those who care about us, because to them we are the universe in so many ways. I continue to forget this, however, in my selfishness, my narcissism, my inability to face reality and my endless focus on what I think I need to be whole, happy and content. I have done a disservice to those I love most, the only people I have. But it can be fixed. I will be home again, and I will manage it differently. I will be my best self. I will be love. I will be a wave all my own. And out here, now, right now, as I lazily circle around bouncing from wave to wave, all of that seems possible, and so the question is, how do I hold onto this feeling, nurture it and be who I am capable of being?

Also though, how do I calm the voice in my head? The one saying, "I would prefer not to" is lingering and disruptive, and I can't quite make it go away. I can be better, I will be better, and that is because I will accept all of this as my fate. I will be Sisyphus, and those moments with Shalla and Joey will be my moment of calm and relief just before the boulder rolls back down the hill and I am off again.

Still, even as I think this, the voice persists. Does this truly have to be my fate? Do I even know? Might I state my preference for something different and my desire to be

something different? Yes, maybe, how? I am no more con-
fident that I could say something to Morg or John than
I was when I could have been honest with Shalla. I may
not be capable of being that guy and I have no idea how
to become that guy. It's not something I can even picture,
not now, not yet. Luckily, I have time to think about it—I
will be in space soon enough.

First though, I need to talk to Lebowski, who I snuck
past so I could hit the waves running, no pause, and no
distractions. I won't be able to do that twice, not if I want
to come back.

As I leave the surf, I see Lebowski sitting cross-legged
in front of his hut, eyes closed and hands folded in his
lap, calm and peaceful. For a moment he looks like he's
floating—his long hair flowing behind him, his beard
wispy and trailing away from his face. I creep up to him
quietly, not wanting to disturb him, and for a moment
I think about just walking by and paying homage when
next I'm here.

I only make it another step though when Lebowski's
arm shoots out at me like a snake, uncoiling and terrify-
ing, his enormous hand instantly wrapping itself around
my ankle in a viselike grip. I am paralyzed with fear: unmoving, unable to move. Lebowski isn't moving either,
just holding me in place, barely breathing, hardly part of
this world even, but holding on with all of his strength.
I look at his arm and consider kicking it with my other
leg. Could I break it if I had to? Maybe, but what if I
could, what then? Would I run through the camp and
keep running until I had safely gotten away? And say I
did, then what, never surf here again, or worse, spend
the rest of my days looking over my shoulder even more
than I already do?

As if on cue, a black helicopter loops by overhead, dipping and pausing, moving on and circling back around, like a vulture, nearly silent like Lebowski, but menacing, always menacing, like Lebowksi is right now, and maybe always was.

Lebowski releases my ankle and turns toward me smiling.

"You weren't going to leave without saying good-bye were you?" Lebowski says smiling.

That is a smile isn't it?

I don't answer immediately, my main desire revolving around wanting to obsessively rub my ankle and chase away the lingering phantom pain and finger prints that are sure to remain.

"It's one thing of course not to stop in on the way out to the surf when the waves are like this, or maybe even if you've had a particularly bad morning, which I think you've had, but to leave without stopping in as well, well that won't work at all, will it?" Lebowski says.

"I-I-I wasn't leaving," I say, leaning over to rub my ankle. "I was just worried about disturbing you."

"Right," Lebowski says, "of course you were, now come here sit, chew some SynthKhat with me, and let's talk before you go."

I take a seat next to Lebowski and grab a handful of SynthKhat from his always plentiful supply. I proceed to chew slowly, as I watch the waves and think about what might be the right thing to say.

"It's hard leaving like this, isn't it?" Lebowski says, looking out across the waves himself. "You're worried about your Terrax on the one hand, but you also just can't bare the idea that you're leaving at all, so soon, everything so unresolved. It's hard, I know, but it's what must be. No questions asked."

"Didn't you once tell me that family came first though, that it was all about family, that I was doing this for my family?" I say, feeling the SynthKhat eating its way into my brain and releasing the thoughts I had blocked out just moments before, "And what if doing this is bad for my family, for me, what if I can't take being away? I couldn't even tell Shalla that my biggest fear was telling her that I was leaving, that the mere idea of it was crippling to me, and so it was easier to hurt her, maybe even destroy what we have by focusing on a jealousy that might exist, but pales in comparison to my feelings about abandoning her and how that impacts her. This opportunity is great, I know that, but it can't be worth it, can it? It can't. I know it can't and the fact is I would just prefer not to do this and I need to say something to John or Morg or whoever can help, right?"

Lebowski is very still and speaks without ever even looking at me.

"I think you may be confused Norrin," Lebowski says reaching out and gently rubbing my shoulder, "I think you believe you have a choice in this, but you don't. You may also believe that you can prefer not to, but you can't. You were chosen, and it means a better life for you and your family if you keep it together. There's no backing out though, regardless. You're in it now. I'm not sure why this isn't more obvious. You're in it, and there's no going backwards, only forwards, for as long as you can, and that's all there is. So go, do what you're supposed to, don't ask questions, and don't make statements about what you would prefer to do, or not to do, it will make sense, everything eventually makes sense, trust in that, and trust in me."

When Lebowski finishes he stands up and so do I. We look at each other, he smiles, and then he wordlessly gives me a hug. After that he walks into his hut and I begin my journey to Arthur Chin and Mars, the memory of Lebowski's smile lingering on the fringes of my still trippy brain, and competing with memories of my father, his leaving and how it never has made any sense to me.

37

I drift into my pod on the train, surrounded as always by ghosts, here today, gone tomorrow, but always going. After my moment in the pod I am exiting into Arthur Chin and drifting toward the main shuttle entrance, relaxed and cool, and ready for security—the full body scans washing over me, probing and prodding like a dream, organs moving and popping, memories and senses lifted and twisted, my mother and her vanilla smell, Al B, performing at Berlin and my dad being marched away, smiling.

Is that defiance, or bemusement, what, and why is he smiling like that?

I never quite registered it like that before, but he's not bothered, never was, no drama and no fear about what is to come. It's odd and something is off about the whole thing, and I would think more about it if I wasn't trying to get through security and I wasn't focused on calm. This time I have none of the anxiety that accompanied me before. I can do this; I may not want to do it, but I will, fearlessly and awesomely and with confidence. No confusion or dread, just goodness and the desire to make it through this, get home and fix everything I would just as soon have destroyed hours earlier.

The police with their fierce grid faces are here again, gripping me and dragging me as I regain my senses and balance. But I remain good and all powerful, focused, and move forward despite my heavy brain, the smell of vanilla everywhere clouding my thinking.

I am brought into a spare, institutional room and dropped into a chair. The E.C.s retreat and there is a moment of silence and peace, which is soon interrupted by movement from somewhere behind me. A body shoots past me, heavy steps, and in a rush, eager, hungry, for something, for me, for information and planets to consume, soaking up all the energy in the room, and excess air. It's okay though, I know what's coming, I am good, and I am present, bring it.

"Hello, Norrin, welcome back," Morg and his smooth baby face say to me from across the table.

He thrusts his hand forward to shake, but I hold back.

"That's fine," Morg says smiling and then leaning back into his chair, "this won't take long anyway."

I remain silent, but lean forward planting my elbows on the table—bring it, I again think to myself, all of it, the worst of it, I'm on a mission.

"You can imagine how sorry we are to send you back out to Mars so quickly," Morg says, "but as my dad always said, sometimes it's better to suck at your job, and you Norrin do not suck, which I guess sucks for you, yes?"

A stab at humor and then what, the hammer? I don't respond.

"Look, its cool, that was a rhetorical question," Morg says. "Here's my actual question, Are you still with us buddy, you got your shit together? Because if you don't we have a problem, and I hate dealing with problems."

I lean back in my chair, all cool all the time.

"All good," I say, "focused on doing my job and getting home."

"Yeah, you sure?" Morg says squinting, trying to assess if there's anything he might be missing.

"Completely," I say.

"Okay then, great, get out of here," Morg says.

"I would prefer not to," I say, "but..."

"You would prefer not to what?" Morg says, jumping in and cutting me off.

"Let me finish Morg, Steven," I say raising my hands, tortured by the feelings I want to keep at bay, and by what I'm about to say, "I would prefer not to go, not to do any of this, but I will, and I will hate it. I will also get back home though, I will make things right and I will be good."

I say this with conviction and I try to believe it. I have to believe it, for now anyway. Morg looks at me for a moment, trying to read me and glean something, anything that helps.

"Okay then, good, get out of here," Morg says.

"That's it?" I say.

"That's it," he says, "if you say you're good, you're good. The package you need to deliver will be waiting for you and you know the drill after that."

I'm good, and now I'm in the Terrax lab and now I am giving them what they need, but I am not present, I am future, and I am looking forward—no looking back, no emotion, no fear, no nothing. Yes, okay, maybe there's a fleeting something as Dr. Thanos is gathering his materials and I know that they are me, will be me, a version of me, but I only let the feeling linger for the briefest of moments. I am done with that, I am going to fix things when I get home and soon I am heading to the shuttle. I am good, and this is my new mantra, goodness in all its forms.

38

"Just lie back, relax, we are preparing to leave," the calming voice says, a voice I have come to love, a voice that will lead me to sleep, and dream as I'm slowly surfing across the universe.

I close my eyes and think about how easy things become when you stop fighting everything and everyone, and wonder that maybe this is what calm is really about—embracing every moment and every relationship for what they are, not what you want them to be?

"You will soon be asleep," the voice continues, now making love to me, lifting me and stroking my senses.

The voice again reminds me of my mother, but today, now, my thoughts shoot from my mother's wispy hair and creamy loving mien to my father, his leaving, that smile. Why didn't I remember that smile before, and what does it mean, about him, about me, and what Joey will remember about this time in his life when someday he looks back as well?

"Close your eyes, relax, think good things, happy things," the voice says sensing, knowing I am not relaxed, can't relax.

I think of Shalla and how I am going to make things right when I get home, reeling in my anxieties, but listening, being there, here, there, and in the moment, she deserves that.

"You're doing great, just take a deep breath," the voice says as the engines on the shuttle come to life with an enormous hiccup of electricity and fire and life, the now familiar scent of ethanol wafting past me and wiping out any lingering vestiges of vanilla as I settle back even further into my bed.

I take a deep breath, and then another, my father's long-ago image fading into the far recesses of my brain as I am drifting away, my eyelids growing heavy and sinking together.

I picture myself out at Kanas Lake, paddling on my kite-board as the sun, all orange and streaky red, rises over the gray waters and gray skies, the endless nothingness stretching farther than I can possibly see.

There is movement below me and around me, a slight hum, some grinding, and there is life, the sense of being pushed from below and above all at once, compressed between invisible hands, flattened and stretched—breathe, think good things, surfing, making love to Shalla, chewing SynthKhat on the beach, holding Joey.

And now there is floating and spinning and spinning and floating, weightless and tired, so very tired, but left with one last thought, one last vapor trail and vestige of the day. I can talk calm and peace with myself, Lebowski and Morg, and I can keep saying I'm cool, and all good. I can pretend that I am managing my feelings, but I'm dying here. That's real, its truth. I am fucking wracked with guilt, and I do not want this, I would prefer not to, and that's that, and it won't change, not now, not ever.

39

There is noise and chaos, metal crunching, twisting and bending. People are screaming somewhere in the darkness and why is everything so dark and smoky? I hear rain, no spraying, something, more screaming, and heat, intense heat on my face, my scalp sizzling, cooking, and the smoke is getting thicker, so dark, and there is a pinging, or clanging, both, my back is sore, heavy, hot, why is it so hot, and why so much smoke?

The floor is moving below me and the ceiling above as well—where, what, why is it do dark, and why can't I move, oh fuck, am I pinned under something?

Where, what the fuck, who, and now I'm coughing, but every contraction is restricted, my eyes are tearing, fuck, more screaming, someone, many, barking orders, indistinguishable. Focus, look, see what, anything, nothing, okay, feel around. Nothing in front or above, nothing really to the sides, wait, what is this, a strap, like a seatbelt? Not pinned, leaning on something, buried, held down, oh shit, I'm still in bed, on the shuttle.

Am I dreaming, no, yes, so conscious though. No, this is real, more crunching, the sick sound of metal twisting into itself—need to move.

Now there is tilting, the shuttle is tilting underneath me, and I am sliding forward, the bed, me, all of it, metal on metal, scratching, grinding and sliding. I am struggling to grab the straps, pulling, picking and clawing at my own chest. The heat on my scalp is building, the sweat dripping onto my forehead, down my nose and onto my chin. I am fighting the momentum, and the sliding, and the straps are in my hand, even as I'm kicking my feet at the approaching wall, which I know is there despite the smoke and the darkness, and the fucking heat.

I undo the straps across my chest, and I swing my legs off of the bed. I pick my way to the door, but it's bent, jammed, unusable and impassable.

I remember that there is an emergency hatch accessible under the bed, and covering my mouth and nose with my sleeve I climb under the bed and look for the latch that will allow me to escape my room and try to figure out what's going on. The latch is where it's supposed to be, but the cover to the hatch is so hot, burning. I move my sleeve from my mouth to my hand and I twist the latch until it gives, a slight spark jumping at my face.

The shaft below the hatch is so tight and hot, and the smoke is everywhere as I start shimmying down the shaft, pushing, inching along, no give, no anything, just the chance to keep moving along, slowly, but with hope on my side.

My legs are dangling, hanging, floating in some kind of space, free and waiting for the rest of me to catch up. Which it does as I slowly move, and try to get my bearings. The smoke is dissipating, the shouting muffled, but present, like white noise, like the ocean slapping against a shore. And now I am dangling, hanging by my hands, trying to see where it is I am dropping and how far, and then I'm just falling into the darkness, free and liberated, yet falling into the unknown.

There is airlessness and soon there is not as I hit the bottom of the shuttle, and crumple into a ball, my legs, back and neck absorbing the shock of the landing, the pain reverberating across me like a sine wave, crushing oscillations that require me to lie down and remember first how to breath, then think and ultimately recall what it means to move at all.

As I lay here, the pain slowly receding into an ache and being absorbed by the floor below me, my other senses start to come back to life.

The screaming is so loud now, as are other noises, sawing, hammering, peeling and grating, metal being crushed and pulled somewhere above me. There is light as well, a sliver of light bisecting me down the middle, splitting me into two inversely matching shadows. I start moving toward the light, first sliding, then crawling on a floor so clearly tilted, and I see that the light is bending its way through a crack on the side of a door on the wall in front of me.

I stand up and feel along the door until I find a knob. I turn it and twist it, but there is no movement, nor give. There is the side of the door though and it is bent, allowing for light and noise, and I place both of my hands on the side of the door and proceed to pull. I expect nothing and I get everything—the door moving in a surprisingly easy fashion, coming at me and crunching as the hinges crack, then crumble and fall at my feet.

I set the door aside, gently, lovingly, as if it will somehow serve its purpose again and I poke my head through the gap I've created.

There is smoke everywhere, the sky grey and bleak, and people are running, some with hoses, some pushing heavy machinery, others with machine guns at the ready, the grids on their faces—shields, blocking out the distractions, the emotions and any sense there is anything but a job to do.

I tentatively lower myself out of the shuttle, happy to feel firm ground below and the crisp air blowing through my hair and cooling my still-steaming skin. I step back into the shadows and as I turn to look at the shuttle I am suddenly wracked with a cough that I cannot shake. It starts somewhere deep in my lungs, causing me to double over, my eyes tearing; one hand on my knee, the other repeatedly slamming me in the face as I try to cover my mouth and each new cough finds a home.

The coughing leaves me light headed and dizzy, momentarily oblivious to the craziness surrounding me. When I am able to stand again I take a look at the shuttle, which remains leaning to its side. Smoke is escaping from a dozen snaking cracks on its exterior, all of it emanating from a massive gash near the nose where a panel is torn in half and hanging by the remaining threads of steel.

The shuttle never got off of the ground. I never left and no one seems to notice that I am standing here watching them try to hose it down and make sense of what has happened.

I start to walk toward the terminal, no one stopping me, no one talking to me, spare snatches of conversation flying around me.

"They stopped maintaining these shuttles the right way a long time ago, we were due."

"No man, it's a terrorist thing, got to be."

"You think? Who, which ones?"

"Does it matter?"

"This was homegrown, it's the nativists. You think you can just exile anyone you want to the fucking wilderness and not expect some blowback?"

"I don't know. These are some pretty junky shuttles man."

I keep walking, no one noticing me, no one talking to me, everyone focused on their job and their paranoia. Things need to be fixed, fixed now.

I walk through a door that takes me into the bowels of Arthur Chin, which is now eerily deserted, the occasional police officer running by, some military-looking types speaking into ear pieces and moving quickly, but otherwise, empty, long halls filled with nothingness.

There is movement behind me, followed by a sharp pain in my shoulder, my head snaps forward, everything going black for a moment. I try to steady myself and look at what's happening behind me. I get the briefest look of a grid, gleaming, and my own startled reflection, before I am shoved again.

"Get moving," the police officer says, "Arthur Chin has been evacuated."

I don't say a word and I just keep walking. I head for the train station. I have no particular plan in mind, just a thought that I cannot shake loose and I would prefer not to—I am going home.

40

I wait outside the pod among the remaining cluster of people looking to exit Arthur Chin. While everyone looks rushed and harried, there is a sense of calm washing over the group as well. We are about to be free of Arthur Chin and whatever went down here. Plus, the train is still running and that means there is normalcy. No one is looking up or around though. They are staring at their feet or the news scroll constantly flashing before us on the Xinhua News Agency news panels evenly aligned along the platform. There is nothing substantial being said about Arthur Chin, it has been closed and evacuated, it will be brief, and everything is fine.

We all begin to enter the pod as the train approaches the station, and we find our spots as the pod latches onto the train. There is a moment as the pod settles into place and the train begins to move where we all shuffle about, angling ourselves this way and that, trying to locate the position that will allow for the least amount of contact with those around us. Soon enough we are heading out of the station and emerging into a world where the sky is still grey, but less bleak, and drabs of sunshine burst through the lingering clouds of smoke that are slowly dissipating as morning fully takes hold and Arthur Chin fades into the background.

No one in the pod is talking, which is not unusual; the norms on the train call for silence and a focus on oneself and one's own business. Still, isn't this a time for conversation, or shared rumination? Are we so jaded about uncertainty and fear that something like this, whatever it is, doesn't faze us? Or is it because we recognize that there is no point, unable as we are to question the Corporation, cowed into silence and apathy, and now unwilling to ask what's going on?

It's some of this I suppose, but as I sit there I realize it's something else as well. This is what shock looks like. You become so focused on moving forward and trying to retain your bearings that you lose yourself in the mundane, concentrating on what you know, and getting home—with that, everything else is blocked out, at least for now and at least until you're ready to truly process it.

So, yes, everyone around me looks relaxed and focused, but they have to be; if they weren't, they would have to face the fact that something happened, something scary, something that may be unknowable, or worse, may be quite knowable, and in the face of that, isn't it so much easier to be like this?

I feel empathy for the people around me, for all of us. This is what it looks like to live today when you are not part of the Corporation or a 1-Percenter. A mix of fear and shock, and the sense that it probably isn't going to get any better. How can it?

I look at the faces in the pod, and I wonder what their stories are. Do they have families as well, and what do they do to support them? Or maybe more accurately, what are they being allowed to do to survive?

They are me, we are all in this together, and though we may not think about it that way, ultimately we are one-in-the-same, the same concerns and the same level of oppression. We are one, we are indistinguishable, and as long as the Corporation prevents any of us from realizing this, or that there may be power in organizing ourselves around this simple idea, they will remain in power and we will remain as we are, pitted against one another and fighting for scraps and dwindling opportunities.

I wonder if this is the shock talking, or if the trauma of the incident has freed me in some way, erasing some of the mental barriers we all must enact to get through the day. I begin to wonder if Morg or someone of his ilk is listening to my thoughts, if they are taking notes, and preparing to talk to me about this when next we meet. I shake my head to make the thoughts go away, and as I do, I am stunned to see someone I recognize standing in the corner.

He is right there, staring out of the window, minding his own business, so close I could be standing next to him in a couple of strides.

For a brief moment I wonder if this is what happens with shock as well?—you start to see things, create ideas and people in your head to compensate for what you cannot bare to face.

I close my eyes and grip the pole next to me. I feel myself starting to spin and I try to hold on, concentrate, and prepare myself to look again.

I open my eyes, and he is still there.

41

This face is so familiar it's blinding, like looking into the sun—the arc of his nose, the slope of his forehead, the shape of his ears and lips, the color of his eyes and the angle of his cheekbones. They are all features I know as well as I know my own, but then of course I do—they are my own. If everyone in this pod is One on some psychic, even spiritual, level, he is more than that, because he is me.

He is my Terrax and we are on the same pod.

It is here, now, that I recognize something else about shock. When we are in shock we go about our business as if there is no other business going on around us. As soon as I see him, everything else, and everywhere else is gone, doesn't matter, the shuttle, the Corporation, the oneness of those of us on the pod. All thoughts of these things have dispersed. I am focused on me, well, I am often focused on me in metaphorical way. But it is me, and it is so similar it's breathtaking.

There is an immediate desire to run to him, touch him, make sure he's real, living, breathing, a warm body like the rest of us. There is even a desire to start questioning him about me, us, me, what does he know that I don't? Does he struggle with the same things that I do? Because you don't have to be in shock to block things out, repress and bury them, our fears and jealousies, the painful memories.

And with that I think back to just hours ago, before all this, and my father, and how different his smile looked. What, what was that, where had that memory existed previously, and is it a real memory, or created by me to cope with something I am just now letting myself think about? Or, has this memory been planted there to mislead me in some way? Is the mere idea that a memory can be planted something the Corporation would do just to trap us in the endless loop of our own thoughts?

And now I'm really spinning, head pounding.

I slam my eyes shut and try to breathe, slowly, one breath, two, three and more, more, and calm, and I'm almost there.

I regain a sense of calm and look back up.

He's gone, vanished, fuck, fuck me, was that all in my head, because maybe that is what shock really is, fabricating our worst and most undesirable objects of confusion. Forcing us to face that which we can never know, always lost halfway through a thought we will never finish?

Because of course this is only partly about the Corporation at best.

What it's actually about is Shalla and trying to make sense of how not to destroy that, us, and knowing I am so very capable of that, and that he is not. The Terrax is the better me. He may not feel like me or hug like me, but he is a better version in so many ways. I apparently am not up for the job of husband. I am limited and weak. And he is not. It's that simple.

However, say the Terrax was still here? He wouldn't have to just haunt me, he could teach me, I could learn from him. What to do and not to do, the things that a father might teach you if there were around to do so. My father is not around though, hasn't been, won't be, and that is not going to change. The Terrax though is, was, and seeing him, that was an opportunity, a chance for something, and now it's just a loss, even if it was never real in the first place, just shock and fear and longing.

The train comes to a halt. We're at our stop. I shake myself out of my reverie and concentrate on leaving the train, not bumping into people, keeping contact to a minimum. As we all spew forth from the train I see him again. He moved. I missed it. And there is still hope.

42

He starts to walk and so do I—same gait, same pace, and same arm swing, which is terribly freaky and terribly cool all at once. I follow him from a distance, scared he will notice me, or just know that something he is part of, or once part of, is near, soon to be reaching out and wanting to connect, or is it re-connect?

As I walk through my neighborhood and along streets I know so well—every turn a memory of some activity with Joey or Shalla, dropping Joey off at school or shopping at Bao—I wonder what my Terrax sees or feels?

Can he know that Joey once tripped on the never-repaired crack in the alley up the street? That he fell to his knees and let out a little cry and then continued on only for us to notice several blocks later how profusely his knee was bleeding and the only way we could distract him after he noticed the blood was to tell him that from this day forward that alley would forever be known as Boo-Boo Alley?

If he does know about that, what does it mean to him? Is it like a file he can access at the moment he needs that information to make a joke or reminisce? Or does he actually feel something? Can he recall the texture of Joey's blood on his fingers? Blood that is his, mine, his, or the fear and awesome responsibility that comes from something even as harmless as a skinned knee that you didn't prevent from occurring, because it makes you wonder what else you will fail to prevent and how there are some things you cannot prevent? Cancer or black helicopters, or the endless array of things that can befall any of us at any time, even when you want to protect your child more than anything in the world?

Can he know that fear and how irrational and paralyzing it is?

Or differently, when he is helping Joey bathe or drying him off or just tucking him in and he sees the little moon-shaped scar on his knee and the stubborn ridge of pinkish scar tissue that never quite goes way, does he have near piercing moments of nostalgia? Flashing back to Joey at three, at two and in Shalla's belly and how incredibly wonderful those ages seem when you are in the middle of them and how you just can't visualize how anything can be better than what you're in the middle of until you reach the next age and the next phase and then you cannot believe you ever felt the way you once did?

Does he know that, and can he feel any of it? Because I can and more profoundly at that with every step.

I'm so lost in these thoughts that I nearly walk into a flash mob forming on the sidewalk before me, a group of black-clad kids, coming together, taunting the black helicopters, the Corporation and the ways of the world they have found themselves part of and subjected to: a world with no work and no promise of a better future.

I swerve to avoid the flash mob as the black helicopter swoops in and in doing so find that I have drifted much closer to my Terrax than I thought I should.

With this realization there is also an immediate sense of panic and confusion and all the things that come with it—the sweat trickling down my back and collecting at the base of my spine and behind my knees; the dry mouth, all cotton and paste; and my head suddenly pounding, a metronome of thumps and collisions.

I am starting to spin into an abyss where I know there

is no return, because that abyss isn't one where I will talk to my Terrax and try to learn from him. That fantasy has been just that, fantasy, but more too. It's been a smoke-screen because I don't want to learn from him—I want him to go away, to leave my memories and my family alone. I want him to stop moving toward my home, and Shalla and Joey who are waiting there, even if they know it isn't quite the same, because they too are caught in their own fantasy. We all are in our own way because that is how we get through the days and months. It's how we survive when we feel abandoned, and I know that feeling, and I don't want to repeat it and it can stop here. I can stop the cycle, and love will be enough.

So now I really am spinning and now my building is so close and now I am thinking that I better slow down a little because I don't have a plan. I've just been moving forward and trying to get home, and I've gotten lost in all these feelings and confusion. But I will need to act soon, somehow, doing something, and there's the door, and maybe, maybe there's movement behind me, and maybe, maybe somewhere above me is the whir of helicopter blades. But all of that is lost to me, because I am walking through the door and I am picking up the pace again. Following him even as he heads to the elevator, and then into the elevator, his back still to me, just steps away.

"Sir!"

I stop abruptly as E.C.'s voice pierces the crazy talking in my brain and as I swivel my head toward E.C., I briefly catch the Terrax's eyes before the elevator doors slam shut.

"Sir," E.C. says more softly this time and more tenderly, almost compassionately.

I look at him and I wonder why he looks so sad, if he truly can look sad, and then there is movement behind me, and it is now, right now, that I realize what being in shock truly is. It's not recognizing that what's happening around you isn't normal. That you think you can treat a situation you're in as though it is the norm, but it isn't, and that's not how it works. In your right mind you would know this and you would recognize what the rules are, what they always are, and how fucked-up everything truly is, but you can't and you don't and as I look at E.C. one more time I fully get this.

Someone, something is behind me, and as I try to turn and face it, there is motion and a blast of pain to the back of my head and then darkness, endless darkness.

43

Aaagh.

Why does my head ache so fucking much? I lift it up, keeping my eyes closed, and try to remember where I am and how I got here, but I don't know where I am or how got here, much less where 'here' is.

There's nothing, no memory of motion or activity.

Wait, cobwebs stir, clouds pass, there is a flicker of something. The shuttle was tilted, and there was smoke, and heat, and I was walking, and Arthur Chin was so empty, except for the police, running, and the pod. I was in the pod. I was shifting, moving, and he was there, the Terrax, and I followed him, and I remembered Joey's knee. Oh, Joey. At first I stayed far away, but then I got close, too close, and E.C. was there.

Why does my head hurt so much though, pounding, nauseating? E.C. piercing my senses, tearing away the final vestiges of shock, getting, no grabbing my attention, and there was a moment, where something made sense, that there are rules, but that I wasn't following them, and then there was motion, and pain, and darkness, and yes, that's it, the last memory, someone hit me in the head.

I reach around to touch the back of my head.

My hair is thick and matted, twisted and wet to the touch in spots and sticky, like molasses. I bring my finger to my nose and sniff it. It smells like death and even though I know what's there, I stick my finger in my mouth and lick it—the taste of copper drifting across my tongue like a sluggish wave.

It's blood, of course it is.

I wonder how long I can keep my eyes closed. I also wonder if I keep them closed forever, if all of this, whatever this is, will go away, stop, and cease to exist, as I now want to cease to exist, becoming nothing, and nowhere at that.

Still, somewhere Shalla and Joey are waiting for me, they have to be, and so I force my eyes open, and with that comes a fleeting image, previously buried until now. There wasn't just the one blow to the head, it was the first of many as I lay there on the floor of the lobby, trying to cover my head, but failing as the barrage of blows blended together and merged with the reflection of the beating I was forced to watch in the ever shiny visage of the police officers' gridlike masks.

"He's coming to," someone says with a metallic burp from some faraway place.

I am in the coffee room at the office, and even though the people in front of me start to come into focus, I am too scared to know what I'm facing and I turn away.

"He looks sick," someone says, also metallically, someone who may be the same guy, though maybe not. My ears are ringing, and for the first time I notice how sore they are as well.

I look again at the people in front of me who are quickly coming into focus.

There are two E.C.s, which initially strikes me as odd as I think about our E.C. and how warm and nonintimidating he is, but then seems much less odd as I recall what we're talking about, robots who serve at our pleasure, and can be programmed to be anything we want them to be.

Dr. Thanos is lurking on the periphery of the room. He looks uncomfortable, pale and nauseous himself. Maybe he's uncomfortable with violence. And maybe he thinks of himself as a man of science, and so being forced to participate in whatever is going on here, and whatever is to come, is more than he ever signed up for.

Directly in front of me is Morg, his baby face fearsome, his smile malevolent. Morg's hands are covered in beautiful leather gloves that have specks of dark, dried blood along the knuckles.

"Morg," I say trying to sound jovial.

Morg doesn't respond at first, instead choosing to motion his right hand, index and middle fingers extended, in my direction from somewhere in the vicinity of his shoulder.

As I stare at his beautiful glove moving to-and-fro in the air, the E.C.s walk over and each grab one of my shoulders, straightening me out until I am as fully erect as I am going to be in my current state. I expect them to walk away, but they don't. Instead they hold me in place, unspeaking, unmoving, the only sound a slight electrical buzz humming emanating from their flawless shells.

Morg walks up to the table and leans forward until we are maybe six inches apart. His breath is hot and sticky, like something newly dead and lying in the street.

"It's Steven," he says.

He leans back slightly onto his heels and as I watch him pull back his right arm, there is no time to react as his right fist slams into my left temple.

"You would prefer not to," he says with disgust as my head violently jerks backwards and I begin to drift away.

"Is he dead?" one of the E.C.s says from somewhere way above me.

"Doubtful," I hear Morg say as I drift away, "but Beck will confirm that."

44

I lift my head.

I am at the table.

Well, of course I am. I was at the table. I did not move. And yet something is different. There are no E.C.s, no Dr. Thanos, just Morg. He's sitting across from me, and he's smiling, just sitting there and waiting for me to say something.

So I do.

"I would prefer not to," I say sluggishly, a mouth full of clay and muck.

"Yes, I know," Morg says, "but that's not going to work. You understand that right?"

"I understand that it doesn't work for you," I say, "but I don't care."

"That's nice," Morg says, "Do you think that Shelley would prefer not to? Of course, but that isn't our problem."

"It could be," I could say, "things could be different, better."

"Bring him in," Morg shouts, jumping up dramatically and awkwardly all at once.

The two E.C.s walk in dragging Shelley by his arms, and he shuffles between them on his old-man legs—a mix of old-man smell, fear, and sadness permeating the room.

"Hey kid," Shelley says, trying to look and sound upbeat.

"Shelley," Morg says, "let me ask you a question, would you prefer not to, you know maybe stop this charade, and just go home?"

"Of course," Shelley says, "more than anything."

"Norrin, do you think we should let him go home?" Morg says.

"Of course," I say, and Shelley smiles.

With that, Morg pulls out a gun and shoots Shelly in the side of the head.

Shelley falls in front of me, hitting the table before dropping onto the floor in a pile—old-man clothes and old-man skin.

I stand up—no plan, no idea what I think or what I'm doing.

"Sit down Norrin," Morg says.

I sit down.

"So here's the plan," Morg says, "John is going to come in here in a moment, and the two of you are going to talk about the date of your next assignment."

"And that's it," I say, wishing I could sound more incredulous than I do.

"That's it," Morg says, "any questions?"

"I guess not," I say.

Morg exits and John walks in. We stare at each other for a moment. He looks pained, though maybe no more so than he usually does.

"I…"

"Yes, I know," John says, "you would prefer not to. I got it. Just go, Norrin. Go find whatever it is you think you need to find, and I will be waiting for you right here, okay?"

"Really?" I say.

"Really," John says, and with that he walks away.

45

There is this moment of quiet when I emerge from the office and back onto BeiShan that makes me think everything is okay or will be. I trot along BeiShan and let myself think that maybe something good happens now, that the worst of it has passed, that things are falling back into place. A feeling that is only reinforced as I get closer to the Simao coffee shop and see Al B standing there as always. He is sentry and oracle—always observing and patiently waiting for things to happen, but also doing enough to ensure that they are happening. That is the kind of guy you want to see at moments like this—they get things done and I need something to get done, even if I'm not entirely clear what it is.

As I approach Al B he is talking into his cell phone, the words lost to the air. He waves me over and hangs up.

"Dude," he says, "what are you doing here?"

"Here, where," I ask, "at Simao with you or in Baidu, or what?"

"You know what I'm saying," Al B says, "I know what's going on, some of it anyway. I also know this isn't the place you ought to be, not that I'm sure where that is. And yet, here you are, so let me repeat my question, what are you doing here, with me, now, why, what?"

"I thought you might be able to help me," I say, "I need to go home."

Al B flinches, composes himself and runs his fingers through his hair. He looks left, right, and skyward, before flipping his dirty hood onto his head.

"You know you can't go home," Al B says.

"Yes, sure," I say, "but does that mean you can't, or won't, help?"

"You never did get it, brother," he says, "none of it."

"I know you're still mad," I say, "and I'm sorry, I get that."

Al B's phone rings, he turns away, answers it, speaks quietly and turns back to me.

"You know, Norrin, that's my point entirely," Al B says, "I was never mad about Shalla, never. You want me to be, maybe you felt trapped and it was easier for you to focus on that shit, but I didn't care, never. You can't go home though bro, you can't. It doesn't work that way. You think you somehow have control over things, when you don't, none of it, and I don't know what else to say, but I'm sorry, really."

"Sorry for what?" I say, but I already know, I can feel the wind picking-up on my neck.

"Sorry for this," Al B says, now beckoning to something off behind me, which I can't yet see, but well know what it is.

"Why?" I say, the whir of the blades coming closer, "If you're not mad at me, why?"

"It's just business brother, and survival, you get that at least, right?" he says turning away from me and raising his hand, asking, begging me to drop it.

Then he is gone, the blades are getting closer, and I am on the move again, and heading home.

46

When I get to my building, I stand there in the shadows looking at my window, waiting for movement, something, anything that will allow me to get Shalla's attention.

When she finally appears though, I know it is impossible. She is with my Terrax. She is with me. She is staring out of the window, his arms around her waist, a small tear lingering on her cheek.

I want to believe she can see me, but if she does she doesn't acknowledge me. Instead she turns to him, me, and strokes his cheek. He smiles and they walk away.

I linger for a moment, but I know that this is why John let me leave, and why Al B said I couldn't go home again.

I have no home.

I head to the lake.

I pick my way through the huts until I reach Lebowski's.

I breathe in the night air.

I grab a kite-board and walk down to the water.

And then I paddle into the darkness.

Acknowledgments

Orphans would not exist without Ray Bradbury, David Mamet, Arthur Miller, Herman Melville, The Ramones, Coen Brothers, Beck, Stan Lee or Walt Disney.

Not that I am great friends with any of the above. Or friends at all actually.

Given this, let me take a moment to express my gratitude to some people I do know—Mark Brand, Joseph Peterson, Mark Heineke, Susan Bean, Sean Allshouse and Adam Lawrence—for without them *Orphans* might just be an idea lacking a home, pages, a cover, and all the things that constitute an actual book.

I am further indebted to Lavinia Ludlow, Amber Sparks, Samuel Sattin, Sal Pane and Sam Weller, superheroes all.

And most finally, much love to my wife, Debbie, my mom, Judy, my brother, Adam, and my boys, Myles and Noah. While I may not write for them, I certainly couldn't do it without them.